AF514088

Marx Machiavelli Chesterton Cooper Emerson Joyce
Abbott Hardy Montaigne Austen
Defoe Melville Haggard Hugo
Christie Carroll Eliot Grimm
Stoker Molière
Wilde Maupassant Byron
Garnett Einstein Fitzgerald Engels Schiller
Goethe Hawthorne Smith Kafka
Cotton Dostoyevsky Hall
Baum Kipling Doyle Willis
Leslie Dumas Henry Nietzsche
Flaubert Turgenev Balzac
Stockton Vatsyayana Crane
Burroughs Whitman Verne
Curtis Tocqueville Gogol Vinci
Homer Widger Tolstoy Busch
Darwin Thoreau
Potter Freud Zola Twain Plato Scott
Lawrence
Kant Jowett Stevenson Dickens
Andersen Cervantes Burton Hesse Harte
London Descartes
Poe Aristotle Wells Voltaire
Hale James Hastings
Bunner Shakespeare Cooke
Richter Chambers Irving
Doré Chekhov da Shaw Wodehouse Benedict
Swift Dante Pushkin Alcott
Newton

tredition®

tredition was established in 2006 by Sandra Latusseck and Soenke Schulz. Based in Hamburg, Germany, tredition offers publishing solutions to authors and publishing houses, combined with worldwide distribution of printed and digital book content. tredition is uniquely positioned to enable authors and publishing houses to create books on their own terms and without conventional manufacturing risks.

For more information please visit: www.tredition.com

TREDITION CLASSICS

This book is part of the TREDITION CLASSICS series. The creators of this series are united by passion for literature and driven by the intention of making all public domain books available in printed format again - worldwide. Most TREDITION CLASSICS titles have been out of print and off the bookstore shelves for decades. At tredition we believe that a great book never goes out of style and that its value is eternal. Several mostly non-profit literature projects provide content to tredition. To support their good work, tredition donates a portion of the proceeds from each sold copy. As a reader of a TREDITION CLASSICS book, you support our mission to save many of the amazing works of world literature from oblivion. See all available books at www.tredition.com.

Project Gutenberg

The content for this book has been graciously provided by Project Gutenberg. Project Gutenberg is a non-profit organization founded by Michael Hart in 1971 at the University of Illinois. The mission of Project Gutenberg is simple: To encourage the creation and distribution of eBooks. Project Gutenberg is the first and largest collection of public domain eBooks.

The Man of the World (1792)

Charles Macklin

Imprint

This book is part of TREDITION CLASSICS

Author: Charles Macklin
Cover design: Buchgut, Berlin – Germany

Publisher: tredition GmbH, Hamburg - Germany
ISBN: 978-3-8424-7584-7

www.tredition.com
www.tredition.de

The intention of the TREDITION CLASSICS series is to make world literature in the public domain available in printed format. Literary enthusiasts and organizations, such as Project Gutenberg, world-wide have scanned and digitally edited the original texts. tredition has subsequently formatted and redesigned the content into a modern reading layout. Therefore, we cannot guarantee the exact reproduction of the original format of a particular historic edition. Please also note that no modifications have been made to the spelling, therefore it may differ from the orthography used today.

INTRODUCTION

During his extraordinarily long career as an actor, Charles Macklin wrote several plays. The earliest is *King Henry VII; or, The Popish Imposter*, a tragedy based on the Perkin Warbeck story, performed at Drury Lane 18 January 1745/6 and published the same year. As the Preface states, it "was design'd as a Kind of Mirror to the present Rebellion"; and it provided the author with a part in which he could express, through the character of Lord Huntley, his own aversion to foreign influences in the land, to "*French* and Priest-rid Weakness" and "Romish Tyranny." This and his succeeding plays were obviously composed to provide parts for himself; so no others were published until he had retired. They were his stock in trade, since Macklin seldom maintained a stable connection with one of the theatres. Instead he appeared now here now there for brief engagements or on special occasions, rather than as a regular member of the company, often carrying his plays with him. Thus a number have survived only in manuscript. The Larpent Collection contains seven,—the tragedy just mentioned, four farces, and two five-act comedies, one of these in three states.[1] This is *The Man of the World* here reproduced for the first time in over a century and a half, despite the opinion expressed by Isaac Reed, in 1782, that "This play, ... in respect to originality, force of mind, and well-adapted satire, may dispute the palm with any dramatic piece that has appeared within the compass of half a century...."[2] Originally it had been performed in Dublin in 1764 under the title *The True-born Scotchman*, but in 1770 the Examiner of Plays in London refused to license it. It was re-submitted in 1779 and again forbidden, but was finally allowed and performed at Covent Garden on 10 May 1781, with the author in the part of Sir Pertinax Macsycophant.

Himself irascible and passionate, Macklin had been the most admired Shylock of his century. His specialty was the performance of character parts, often dialect roles, either broadly comic or cruel and ironic. The central figure of this, his best comedy, is such a part. It combines those features that the author could portray so effectively, the broad dialect, the callous selfishness, the hypocrisy, the passionate resistance to all appeals to sentiment and the imperviousness to affection. One can detect in the creation strong resemblances to Macklin's interpretation of Shylock, something of Sir Giles Overreach, who was also known to eighteenth-century play-goers, and possibly of Tartuffe. In his resolute defiance of the conventions of comedy of sensibility, Macklin resisted the pressure to allow Sir Pertinax to soften in the end and terminate the play on a note of happy reconciliation and family harmony.

In thus preserving the toughness of Sir Pertinax consistently to the end, Macklin remained true to the tradition of critical, satiric comedy that he had been bred in but that by this time had almost disappeared. Protesting against the refusal of a license for his play, in 1779, Macklin composed a defense of satiric comedy. He insists upon the reformatory function of comedy and upon the satiric method of performing this task. "The business of the Stage," he says, "is to correct vice, and laugh at folly ... This piece is in support of virtue, morality, decency, and the Laws of the Land: it satirizes both public and private venality, and reprobates inordinate passions and tyrannical conduct in a parent ... Now, with regard to my comedy is it not just and salutary that the subtilty [*sic*], pride, insolence, cunning, and the thorough-paced villany [*sic*] of a backbiting Scotchman should be ridiculed? What a wretched state the Comic Muse and the Stage would be reduced to, were the prohibition of laughing at the corruption and other vices of the age to prevail!"[3] True the Comic Muse, long sick, as Garrick said in his prologue to *She Stoops to Conquer*, had almost died, though farces had done something to sustain her. Fielding's and Garrick's little satires had largely avoided sentiment; and the personal, often gross farces of Foote had continued to use ridicule. But even these lack the forceful pertinacity of Macklin's denunciation of hypocrisy and vice. It is perhaps too bad that he fell so far into caricature in the portraits of Lord Lumbercourt and his daughter, that the main love stories do smack of sensibility, and that he turned his hero into a mouthpiece for the opposition to the Tory ministries of the early years of George III. And it is perhaps true that all the characters, including Sir Pertinax, are more true to the theatre than to the actual life of the last quarter of the eighteenth century. Still, Sir Pertinax is vigorous, and the author's position is unmistakable.

The earliest portion of *The Man of the World* in the Larpent Collection is a passage in the fourth act of *The School for Husbands*, performed at Covent Garden as *The Married Libertine* on 28 January 1761, twenty years before *The Man of the World* was finally presented in London. Elsewhere I have compared the three complete versions submitted to the Examiner and have shown why the Lord Chamberlain could not permit it to be licensed.[4]

The Man of the World was first published in England, with Macklin's farce *Love a la Mode*, by subscription, in a handsome quarto. Facing the title-page is a portrait of the author, "in his 93.^d Year," engraved by John Condé after Opie, for which the trustees of the fund paid 25 guineas. Preceding the text of the play are the list of subscribers, which contains many eminent names, an "Advertisement from the Editor," explaining the occasion and method of publication and giving an account of the handling of the fund by the trustees, and a dedication to Lord Camden, dated 10 December 1792, and signed by Macklin, though one rather suspects that Arthur Murphy had a hand in its composition. These pieces of front matter have been omitted from the present reproduction as containing nothing material to the reading or interpretation of the play. The *Dramatis Personae* follow, and the text begins with signature B page 1, and runs to signature K2^{V}. *Love a la Mode*, not reprinted here, then follows, with separate title-page and pagination.

Dougald MacMillan

The University of North Carolina

Notes to the Introduction

[Footnote 1: See *Catalogue of the Larpent Plays in the Huntington Library* (1939), Nos. 55, 58, 64, 96, 184, 274, 311, 500, 558.]

[Footnote 2: *Biographia Dramatica* (1812), III, 15.]

[Footnote 3: Quoted by Edward Abbot Parry, *Charles Macklin* (1891), p. 179.]

[Footnote 4: See *The Huntington Library Bulletin*, No. 10 (October, 1936), pp. 79-101.]

THE MAN OF THE WORLD.

A COMEDY.

BY

MR. CHARLES MACKLIN.

AS PERFORMED AT THE

THEATRES-ROYAL, DRURY-LANE AND COVENT-GARDEN.

Dramatis Personæ.

COVENT-GARDEN.

Men.

***SIR PERTINAX MACSYCOPHANT,* MR. WILSON. *EGERTON,* MR. LEWIS. *LORD LUMBERCOURT* MR. THOMPSON. *SIDNEY,* MR. AICKIN. *MELVILLE,* MR. HULL. *COUNSELLOR PLAUSIBLE* MR. CUBITT. *SERJEANT EITHERSIDE,* MR. MACREADY. *SAM,* MR. LEDGER. *JOHN,* MR. ROCK *TOMLINS,* MR. EVATT.**

Women

***LADY MACSYCOPHANT* MISS. PLATT. *LADY RODOLPHA LUMBERCOURT,* MRS. POPE. *CONSTANTIA,* MRS. MOUNTAIN. *BETTY HINT,* MRS. ROCK. *NANNY,* MRS. DEVERETT.**

THE MAN OF THE WORLD.

ACT I. SCENE I.

A Library. Enter BETTY *and* SAM.

Betty. The Postman is at the gate, Sam; pray step and take in the letters.

Sam. John the gardener is gone for them, Mrs. Betty.

Bet. Bid John bring them to me, Sam: tell him I am here in the Library.

Sam. I'll send him to your ladyship in a crack, madam. [*Exit.*

Enter NANNY.

Nan. Miss Constantia desires to speak to you, Mrs. Betty.

Bet. How is she now? any better, Nanny?

Nan. Something; but very low spirited still. I verily believe it is as you say.

Bet. O! I would take my book oath of it. I can not be deceived in that point, Nanny.—Ay, ay, her business is done, she is certainly breeding, depend upon it.

Nan. Why so the housekeeper thinks too.

Bet. Nay, I know the father—the man that ruined her.

Nan. The deuce you do?

Bet. As sure as you are alive, Nanny;—or I am greatly deceived,—and yet—I can't be deceived neither.—Was not that the cook that came gallopping so hard over the common just now?

Nan. The same:—how very hard he gallopped;—-he has been but three quarters of an hour, he says, coming from Hyde Park Corner.

Bet. And what time will the family be down?

Nan. He has orders to have dinner ready by five; there are to be lawyers and a great deal of company here—he fancies there is to be a private wedding to night between our young Master Charles and Lord Lumbercourt's Daughter, the Scotch lady, who he says is just come post from Bath in order to be married to him.

Bet. Ay, ay—Lady Rodolpha—nay, like enough—for I know it has been talked of a good while;—well, go tell Miss Constantia that I will be with her immediately.

Nan. I shall, Mrs. Betty. [*Exit.*

Bet. Soh! I find they all believe the impertinent creature is breeding—that's pure! it will soon reach my lady's ears, I warrant.

Enter JOHN.

Well, John, ever a letter for me?

John. No, Mrs. Betty, but here is one for Miss Constantia.

Bet. Give it me.—Hum!—my lady's hand.

John. And here is one which the postman says is for my young master—but it's a strange direction. [*reads.*] '*To* Charles Egerton, *Esq.*'

Bet. O! yes, yes,—that is for Master Charles, John:—for he has dropped his father's name of Macsycophant, and has taken up that of Egerton—the parliament has ordered it.

John. The parliament!—pr'ythee, why so, Mrs. Betty?

Bet. Why you must know, John, that my lady, his mother, was an Egerton by her father:—she stole a match with our old master, for which all her family on both sides have hated Sir Pertinax and the whole crew of the Macsycophants ever since.

John. Except Master Charles, Mrs. Betty.

Bet. O! they dote upon him, though he is a Macsycophant—he is the pride of all my lady's family:—and so, John,—my lady's uncle, Sir Stanley Egerton dying an old bachelor, and, as I said before, mortally hating our old master, and all the crew of the Macsycophants, left his whole estate to Master Charles, who was his godson,—but on condition that he should drop his father's name of Macsycophant, and take up that of Egerton—and that is the reason, John, why the parliament has made him change his name.

John. I am glad that Master Charles has got the estate, however—for he is a sweet tempered gentleman.

Bet. As ever lived:—but come, John, as I know you love Miss Constantia, and are fond of being where she is—I will make you happy;—you shall carry her letter to her.

John. Shall I, Mrs. Betty?—I am very much obliged to you.—Where is she?

Bet. In the housekeeper's room settling the dessert.—Give me Mr. Egerton's letter, and I'll leave it on the table in his dressing room. I see it's from his brother Sandy.—So,—now go and deliver your letter to your sweetheart, John.

John. That I will;—and I am much beholden to you for the favour of letting me carry it to her:—for though she should never have me, yet I shall always love her, and wish to be near her, she is so sweet a creature.—Your servant, Mrs. Betty. [*Exit.*

Bet. Your servant, John. Ha, ha, ha! poor fellow! he perfectly dotes on her—and daily follows her about with nosegays and fruit and the first of every thing in the season.—Ay, and my young Master Charles too is in as bad a way as the gardener:—in short—every body loves her,—and that's one reason why I hate her.—For my part, I wonder what the deuce the men see in her—a creature that was taken in for charity.—I am sure she's not so handsome.—I wish she was out of the family once:—if she was, I might then stand a chance of being my lady's favourite myself;—ay, and perhaps of getting one of my young masters for a sweetheart,—or at least the chaplain: but as to him, there would be no such great catch if I should get him. I will try for him however,—and my first step shall be to tell the doctor all I have discovered about Constantia's intrigues with her spark at Hadley.—Yes,—that will do,—for the doctor loves to talk with me,—loves to hear *me* talk too,—and I verily believe—he, he, he!—that he has a sneaking kindness for me,—and this story will make him have a good opinion of my honesty,—and that, I am sure, will be one step towards— —O! bless me,—here he comes,—and my young master with him.— I'll watch an opportunity to speak to him as soon as he is alone,—for I will blow her up I am resolved,—as great a favourite and as cunning as she is. [*Exit.*

Enter EGERTON *in great warmth and emotion;*
SIDNEY *following, as in conversation.*

Sid. Nay, dear Charles, but why are you so impetuous?—why do you break from me so abruptly?

Eger. [With great warmth.] I have done, sir,—you have refused.—I have nothing more to say upon the subject.—I am satisfied.

Sid. [With a glow of tender friendship.] Come, come—correct this warmth,—it is the only weak ingredient in your nature, and you ought to watch it carefully. If I am wrong,—I will submit without reserve;—but consider the nature of your request—and how it would affect me:—from your earliest youth, your father has honoured me with the care of your education, and the general conduct of your mind; and, however singular and morose his temper may be to others,—to me—he has ever been respectful and liberal.—I am now under his roof too,—and because I will not abet an unwarrantable passion by an abuse of my sacred character, in marrying you beneath your rank,—and in direct opposition to your father's hopes and happiness,—you blame me—you angrily break from me—and call me unkind.

Eger. [With tenderness and conviction.] Dear Sidney,—for my warmth I stand condemned: but for my marriage with Constantia, I think I can justify it upon every principle of filial duty,—honour,—and worldly prudence.

Sid. Only make that appear, Charles, and you know you may command me.

Eger. [*With great filial regret.*] I am sensible how unseemly it appears in a son to descant on the unamiable passions of a parent;—but, as we are alone, and friends,—I cannot help observing in my own defence,—that when a father will not allow the use of reason to any of his family—when his pursuit of greatness makes him a slave abroad—only to be a tyrant at home,—when a narrow partiality to Scotland, on every trivial occasion, provokes him to enmity even with his wife and children, only because they dare give a national preference where they think it most justly due;—and when, merely to gratify his own ambition, he would marry his son into a family he detests,—[*great warmth.*] sure, Sidney, a son thus circumstanced (from the dignity of human reason and the feelings of a loving heart) has a right—not only to protest against the blindness of a parent, but to pursue those measures that virtue and happiness point out.

Sid. The violent temper of Sir Pertinax, I own, cannot be defended on many occasions, but still—your intended alliance with Lord Lumbercourt—

Eger. [*With great impatience.*] O! contemptible!—a trifling, quaint, haughty, voluptuous, servile tool,—the mere lackey of party and corruption; who, for the prostitution of near thirty years and the ruin of a noble fortune, has had the despicable satisfaction, and the infamous honour—of being kicked up and kicked down—kicked in and kicked out,— just as the insolence, compassion, or convenience of leaders predominated:—and now—being forsaken by all parties, his whole political consequence amounts to the power of franking a letter, and the right honourable privilege of not paying a tradesman's bill.

Sid. Well, but, dear Charles, you are not to wed my lord,—but his daughter.

Eger. Who is as disagreeable to me for a companion, as her father for a friend, or an ally.

Sid. What—her Scotch accent, I suppose, offends you?

Eger. No, upon my honour—not in the least,—I think it entertaining in her;—but were it otherwise—in decency—and indeed in national affection (being a Scotchman myself), I can have no objection to her on that account,—besides, she is my near relation.

Sid. So I understand. But pray, Charles, how came Lady Rodolpha, who, I find, was born in England, to be bred in Scotland?

Eger. From the dotage of an old, formal, obstinate, stiff, rich, Scotch grandmother, who, upon a promise of leaving this grandchild all her fortune, would have the girl sent to her to Scotland, when she was but a year old, and there has she been ever since, bred up with this old lady in all the vanity and unlimited indulgence that fondness and admiration could bestow on a spoiled child—a fancied beauty and a pretended wit.

Sid. O! you are too severe upon her.

Eger. I do not think so, Sidney; for she seems a being expressly fashioned by nature to figure in these days of levity and dissipation:— her spirits are inexhaustible: her parts strong and lively; with a sagacity that discerns, and a talent not unhappy in painting out the weak side of whatever comes before her:—but what raises her merit to the highest pitch in the laughing world is her boundless vanity and spirits in the exertion of those talents, which often render her much more ridiculous than the most whimsical of the characters she exposes—[*in a tone of friendly affection.*] and is *this* a woman fit to make *my* happiness?— *this* the partner that Sidney would recommend to me for life?—to *you*, who best know me, I appeal.

Sid. Why, Charles, it is a delicate point,—unfit for *me* to determine—besides, your father has set his heart upon the match.

Eger. [*Impatiently.*] All that I know:—but still I ask and insist upon your candid judgment,—is she the kind of woman that you think could possibly contribute to my happiness? I beg you will give me an explicit answer.

Sid. The subject is disagreeable;—but, since I must speak,—I do not think she is.

Eger. [*a start of friendly rapture.*] I know you do not; and I am sure you never will advise the match.

Sid. I never did. I never will.

Eger. [*With a start of joy*.] You make me happy,—which I assure you I never could be with your judgment against me in this point.

Sid. And yet, Charles, give me leave to observe, that Lady Rodolpha, with all her ridiculous and laughing vanity, has a goodness of heart, and a kind of vivacity that not only entertains,—but upon seeing her two or three times, she improves upon you; and when her torrent of spirits abates, and she condescends to converse gravely—you really like her.

Eger. Why ay! she is sprightly, good humoured, and, though whimsical, and often too high in her colouring of characters, and in the trifling business of the idle world,—yet I think she has principles, and a good heart,—[*with a glow of conjugal tenderness*.] but in a partner for life, Sidney, (you know your own precept, and your own judgment)—affection, capricious in its nature, must have something even in the external manners,—nay in the very mode, not only of beauty, but of virtue itself— which both heart and judgment must approve, or our happiness in that delicate point cannot be lasting.

Sid. I grant it.

Eger. And that mode,—that amiable essential I never can meet—but in Constantia. You sigh.

Sid. No. I only wish that Constantia had a fortune equal to yours. But pray, Charles, suppose I had been so indiscreet as to have agreed to marry you to Constantia—would *she* have consented, think you?

Eger. That I cannot say positively,—but I suppose so.

Sid. Did you never speak to her upon that subject then?

Eger. In general terms only;—never directly requested her consent in form,—[*he starts into a warmth of amorous resolution*.] but I will this very moment—for I have no asylum from my father's arbitrary design, but my Constantia's arms.—Pray do not stir from hence:—I will return instantly. I know she will submit to your advice—and I am sure you will persuade her to my wish, as my life, my peace, my earthly happiness, depend on my Constantia. [*Exit*.

Sid. Poor Charles! he little dreams that I love Constantia too,—but to what degree I knew not myself, till he importuned me to join their hands.—Yes—I love—but must not be a rival; for he is dear to me as fraternal affinity:—my benefactor—my friend—and that name is sacred:— it is our better self; and ever ought to be preferred;—for the man who gratifies his passions at the expence of his friend's happiness, wants but a head to contrive—for he has a heart capable of the blackest vice.

Enter BETTY, *running up to* Sidney.

Bet. I beg pardon for my intrusion, sir. I hope, sir, I do not disturb your reverence!

Sid. Not in the least, Mrs. Betty.

Bet. I humbly beg you will excuse me, sir:—but I wanted to break my mind to your honour—about a scruple that lies upon my conscience:—and indeed I should not have presumed to trouble you, sir, but that I know you are my young master's friend,—and my old master's friend,—and indeed—a friend to the whole family: [*runs up to him and curtsies very low*.] for to give you your due, sir, you are as good a preacher as ever went into a pulpit.

Sid. Ha, ha, ha! do you think so, Mrs. Betty?

Bet. Ay, in truth do I; and as good a gentleman too as ever came into a family, and one that never gives a servant a bad word, nor that does any one an ill turn neither behind their back, nor before their face.

Sid. Ha, ha, ha! why you are a mighty well spoken woman, Mrs. Betty, and I am mightily beholden to you for your good character of me.

Bet. Indeed, sir, it is no more than you deserve, and what all the world and all the servants say of you.

Sid. I am much obliged to them, Mrs. Betty.—But pray what are your commands with me?

Bet. Why, I'll tell you, sir:—to be sure I am but a servant, as a body may say—and every tub should stand upon its own bottom;—but—[*she takes hold of him familiarly, looks first about cautiously, and speaks in a low familiar tone of great secrecy*.] my young master is now in the china room in close conference with Miss Constantia;—I know what they are about—but that is no business of mine—and therefore I made bold to listen a little—because you know, sir, one would be sure—before one took away any body's reputation.

Sid. Very true, Mrs. Betty,—very true indeed.

Bet. O! heavens forbid that I should take away any young woman's good name—unless I had a good reason for it; but, sir, [*with great solemnity*.] if I am in this place alive, as I listened, with my ear close to the door,—I heard my young master ask Miss Constantia the plain marriage question—upon which I started—and trembled—nay my very conscience stirred within me so,—that I could not help peeping through the key-hole.

Sid. Ha, ha, ha! and so your conscience made you peep through the key-hole, Mrs. Betty?

Bet. It did indeed, sir:—and there I saw my young master upon his knees—lord bless us—and what do you think he was doing?—kissing her hand as if he would eat it—and protesting—and assuring her—he knew that you, sir, would consent to the match—and then the tears ran down her cheeks as fast—

Sid. Ay!

Bet. They did indeed. I would not tell your reverence a lie for the world.

Sid. I believe it, Mrs. Betty—and what did Constantia say to all this?

Bet. O!—O! she is sly enough; she looks as if butter would not melt in her mouth; but all is not gold that glitters; smooth water, you know, sir, runs deepest:—I am sorry my young master makes such a fool of himself— but—um!—take my word for it, he is not the man,—for though she looks as modest as a maid at a christening—[*hesitating*.] yet—ah!—when sweethearts meet—in the dusk of the evening—and stay together a whole hour—in the dark grove—and embrace—and kiss—and weep at parting,—why then you know, sir, it is easy to guess all the rest.

Sid. Why did Constantia meet any body in this manner?

Bet. [*Starting with surprise.*] O! heavens!—I beg, sir, you will not misapprehend me; for I assure you I do not believe they did any harm—that is, not in the grove—at least, not when I was there;—and she may be honestly married for aught I know.—O! lud! sir,—I would not say an ill thing of Miss Constantia for the world,—for to be sure she is a good creature:—'tis true, my lady took her in for charity, and indeed has bred her up to the music and figures;—ay, and reading all the books about Homer—and Paradise—and Gods and Devils,—and every thing in the world,— as if she had been a dutchess: but some people are born with luck in their mouths, and then—as the saying is—you may throw them into the sea— [*deports herself most affedtedly.*] but—if I had had dancing masters— and music masters—and French Mounseers to teach me—I believe I might have read the globes, and the maps,—and have danced,—and have been as clever as other folks.

Sid. Ha, ha, ha! no doubt on it, Mrs. Betty;—but you mentioned something of a dark walk,—kissing,—a sweetheart and Constantia.

Bet. [*Starts into a cautious hypocrisy.*] O! lud! sir—I don't know any thing of the matter: she may be very honest for aught I know: I only say, that they did meet in the dark walk,—and all the servants observe that Miss Constantia wears her stays very loose—looks very pale—is sick in a morning, and after dinner: and, as sure as my name is Betty Hint, something has happened that I won't name,—but—nine months hence—a certain person in this family may ask me to stand godmother, for I think I know what's what, when I see it as well as another.

Sid. No doubt you do, Mrs. Betty.

Bet. [*Cries, turns up her eyes, and acts a most friendly hypocrisy.*] I do, indeed, sir. I am very sorry for Miss Constantia. I never thought she would have taken such courses—for in truth I love her as if she was my own sister; and though all the servants say that she is breeding—yet, for my part, I don't believe it; but—one must speak according to one's conscience, you know, sir.

Sid. O! I see you do.

Bet. [*Going and returning.*] I do indeed, sir: and so your servant, sir—but—I hope your worship won't mention my name in this business;—or that you had any *item* from me.

Sid. I shall not, Mrs. Betty.

Bet. For, indeed, sir, I am no busybody, nor do I love fending nor proving; and, I assure you, sir, I hate all tittling and tattling, and gossiping and backbiting, and taking away a person's good name.

Sid. I observe you do, Mrs. Betty.

Set. I do indeed, sir. I am the farthest from it in the world.

Sid. I dare say you are.

Bet. I am indeed, sir, and so your humble servant.

Sid. Your servant, Mrs. Betty.

Bet. [*Aside, in great exultation.*] So! I see he believes every word I say,—that's charming. I'll do her business for her I am resolved. [*Exit.*

Sid. What can this ridiculous creature mean by her dark walk,—her private spark, her kissing, and all her slanderous insinuations against Constantia, whose conduct is as unblamable as innocence itself? I see envy is as malignant in a paltry waiting wench, as in the vainest or most ambitious lady of the court.—It is always an infallible mark of the basest nature; and merit in the lowest, as well as in the highest station, must feel the shaft of envy's constant agents—falsehood and slander.

Enter SAM.

Sam. Sir, Mr. Egerton and Miss Constantia desire to speak with you in the china room.

Sid. Very well, Sam. [*Exit* Sam.] I will not see them.—What is to be done? inform his father of his intended marriage,—no—that must not be;— for the overbearing nature and ambitious policy of Sir Pertinax would exceed all bounds of moderation; for he is of a sharp, shrewd, unforgiving nature.—He has banished one son already, only for daring to differ from his judgment concerning the merits of a Scotch and an English historian.— But this young man must not marry Constantia.—Would his mother were here! She, I suppose, knows nothing of his indiscretion:—but she shall, the moment she comes hither. I know it will offend him; no matter: it is our duty to offend,—when that offence saves the man we love from a precipitate action, which the world must condemn, and his own heart, perhaps, upon reflection, for ever repent: yes,—I must discharge the duty of my function, and of a friend,—though I am sure to lose the man, whom I intend to serve. [*Exit.*

END OF THE FIRST ACT.

ACT II. SCENE I.

Enter CONSTANTIA *and* EGERTON.

Con. Mr. Sidney is not here, sir.

Eger. I assure you I left him, and begged he would stay till I returned.

Con. His prudence, you see, sir, has made him retire; therefore we had better defer the subject till he is present; in the mean time, sir, I hope you will permit me to mention an affair that has greatly alarmed and perplexed me: I suppose you guess what it is.

Eger. I do not, upon my word.

Con. That is a little strange.—You know, sir, that you and Mr. Sidney did me the honour of breakfasting with me this morning in my little study.

Eger. We had that happiness, madam.

Con. Just after you left me, upon opening my book of accompts, which lay in the drawer of the reading desk, to my great surprise, I there found this case of jewels, containing a most elegant pair of earrings, a necklace of great value, and two bank bills in this pocket book, the mystery of which, sir, I presume you can explain.

Eger. I can.

Con. They were of your conveying then?

Eger. They were, madam.

Con. I assure you they startled and alarmed me.

Eger. I hope it was a kind alarm;—such as blushing virtue feels, when, with her hand, she gives her heart and last consent.

Con. It was not indeed, sir.

Eger. Do not say so, Constantia: come—be kind at once;—my peace and worldly bliss depend upon this moment.

Con. What would you have me do?

Eger. What love and virtue dictate.

Con. O! sir, experience but too severely proves, that such unequal matches as ours, never produce aught but contempt and anger in parents, censure from the world, and a long train of sorrow and repentance in the wretched parties,—which is but too often entailed upon their hapless issue.

Eger. But that, Constantia, can not be our case: my fortune is independent and ample,—equal to luxury and splendid folly. I have a right to choose the partner of my heart,

Con. But I have not, sir.—I am a dependant on my lady,—a poor, forsaken, helpless orphan—your benevolent mother found me—took me to her bosom—and there supplied my parental loss—with every tender care— indulgent dalliance, and with all the sweet persuasion that maternal fondness, religious precept, polished manners, and hourly example could administer—she fostered me: [*weeps.*] and shall I now turn viper,—and with black ingratitude sting the tender heart that thus hath cherished me? shall I seduce her house's heir, and kill her peace?—No—though I loved to the mad extreme of female fondness; though every worldly bliss that woman's vanity or man's ambition could desire, followed the indulgence of my love—and all the contempt and misery of this life, the denial of that indulgence—I would discharge my duty to my benefactress—my earthly guardian, my more than parent.

Eger. My dear Constantia, your prudence, your gratitude, and the cruel virtue of your self-denial, do but increase my love, my admiration, and my misery.

Con. Sir, I must beg you will give me leave to return these bills and jewels.

Eger. Pray do not mention them:—sure my kindness and esteem may be indulged so far without suspicion or reproach.—I beg you will accept of them,—nay—I insist.

Con. I have done, sir: my station here is to obey.—I know, sir, they are gifts of a virtuous mind—and mine shall convert them to the tenderest, and most grateful use.

Eger. Hark! I hear a coach:—it is my father.—Dear girl, retire and compose yourself.—I will send Sidney and my lady to you, and by their judgment we will be directed: will that satisfy you?

Con. I can have no will but my lady's.—With your leave I will retire; I would not see her in this confusion.

Eger. Dear girl, adieu! and think of love, of happiness, and the man who never can be blest without you. [*Exit* Constantia.

Enter SAM.

Sam. Sir Pertinax and my lady are come, sir,—and my lady desires to speak with you in her own room:—oh! here she is, sir. [*Exit.*

Enter Lady MACSYCOPHANT.

Lady Mac. [*In great confusion and distress.*] Dear child, I am glad to see you: why did you not come to town yesterday to attend the levee? your father is incensed to the uttermost at your not being there.

Eger. [*With great warmth.*] Madam, it is with extreme regret I tell you, that I can no longer be a slave to his temper, his politics, and his scheme of marrying me to this woman,—therefore you had better consent at once to my going out of the kingdom, and my taking Constantia with me, for without her I never can be happy.

Lady Mac. As you regard my peace, or your own character, I beg you will not be guilty of so rash a step.—You promised me you never would marry her without my consent.—I will open it to your father.—Pray, dear Charles, be ruled:—let me prevail.

Sir PERTINAX. [*Without, in great anger.*]

Sir Per. Sir, wull ye do as ye are bid—and haud your gab, you rascal.— You are so full of gab, you scoundrel.—Take the chesnut gelding, I say, and return to town directly, and see what is become of my Lord Lumbercourt.

Lady Mac. Here he comes.—I will get out of his way.—But I beg, Charles, while he is in this ill humour that you will not oppose him, let him say what he will—when his passion is a little cool, I will return, and try to bring him to reason: but do not thwart him.

Eger. Madam, I will not. [*Exit* Lady Mac.

Sir Per. [*Witbout.*] Here, you Tomlins, where is my son Egerton?

Tom. [*Without.*] In the library, sir.

Sir Per. [*Without.*] As soon as the lawyers come, be sure bring me word, [*Enters with great haughtiness, and in anger.* EGERTON *bows two or three times most submissively low.*] Weel, sir!—vary weel!—vary weel!— are nat ye a fine spark? are nat ye a fine spark, I say?—ah! you are a— so you wou'd not come up till the levee?

Eger. Sir, I beg your pardon—but—I was not very well; besides I did not think my presence there was necessary.

Sir Per. [*Snapping him up.*] Sir, it was necessary—I tauld you it was necessary—and, sir, I must now tell you, that the whole tenor of your conduct is most offensive.

Eger. I am sorry you think so, sir; I am sure I do not intend to offend you.

Sir Per. I care not what you intend.—Sir, I tell you, you do offend. What is the meaning of this conduct, sir? neglect the levee!—'sdeath, sir, you—what is your reason, I say, for thus neglecting the levee, and disobeying my commands?

Eger. [*With a stifled, filial resentment.*] Sir, I am not used to levees: nor do I know how to dispose of myself,—nor what to say, or do, in such a situation.

Sir Per. [*With a proud, angry resentment.*] Zounds! sir, do you nat see what others do? gentle and simple,—temporal and spiritual,—lords, members, judges, generals, and bishops,—aw crowding, bustling, and pushing foremost intill the middle of the circle, and there waiting, watching, and striving to catch a look or a smile fra the great mon,— which they meet—wi' an amicable reesibility of aspect—a modest cadence of body, and a conciliating co-operation of the whole mon,—which expresses an officious promptitude for his service—and indicates, that they luock upon themselves as the suppliant appendages of his power, and the enlisted Swiss of his poleetical fortune;—this, sir, is what you ought to do,—and this, sir, is what I never once omitted for these five and thraty years,—let who would be minister.

Eger. [*Aside.*] Contemptible!

Sir Per. What is that you mutter, sir?

Eger. Only a slight reflection, sir, not relative to you.

Sir Per. Sir, your absenting yourself fra the levee at this juncture is suspeecious; it is looked upon as a kind of disaffection,—and aw your countrymen are highly offended at your conduct,——for, sir, they do not look upon you as a friend or a well-wisher either to Scotland or Scotchmen.

Eger. [*With a quick warmth.*] Then, sir, they wrong me, I assure you,— but pray, sir, in what particular can I be charged—either with coldness or offence to my country?

Sir Per. Why, sir, ever since your mother's uncle, Sir Stanly Egerton, left you this three thousand pounds a year, and that you have, in compliance with his will, taken up the name of Egerton, they think you are grown proud;—that you have estranged yourself fra the Macsycophants—have associated with your mother's family—with the opposeetion, and with those who do not wish well till Scotland;——besides, sir, the other day, in a conversation at dinner at your cousin Campbel M'Kenzie's, before a whole table-full of your ain relations, did not you publicly wish a total extinguishment of aw party, and of aw national distinctions whatever, relative to the three kingdoms?—[*With great anger.*] And you blockhead— was that a prudent wish before so many of your ain countrymen?—or was it a filial language to hold before me?

Eger. Sir, with your pardon, I cannot think it unfilial or imprudent. [*With a most patriotic warmth.*] I own I do wish—most ardently wish for a total extinction of all party: particularly—that those of English, Irish, and Scotch might never more be brought into contest or competition, unless, like loving brothers, in generous emulation, for one common cause.

Sir Per. How, sir! do you persist? what!—would you banish aw party, and aw distinction between English, Irish, and your ain countrymen?

Eger. [*With great dignity of spirit.*] I would, sir.

Sir Per. Then damn you, sir,—you are nai true Scot.—Ay, sir, you may look as angry as you will,—but again I say—you are nai true Scot.

Eger. Your pardon, sir, I think he is the true Scot, and the true citizen, who wishes equal justice to the merit and demerit of every subject of Great Britain; amongst whom I know but of two distinctions.

Sir Per. Weel sir, and what are those? what are those?

Eger. The knave and the honest man.

Sir Per. Pshaw! rideeculous.

Eger. And he, who makes any other—let him be of the North, or of the South—of the East, or of the West—in place, or out of place—is an enemy to the whole, and to the virtues of humanity.

Sir Per. Ay, sir, this is your brother's impudent doctrine—for the which, I have banished him for ever fra my presence, my heart, and my fortune.—Sir, I will have no son of mine, because truly he has been educated in an English seminary, presume, under the mask of candour, to speak against his native land, or against my principles.

Eger. I never did—nor do I intend it.

Sir Per. Sir, I do not believe you—I do not believe you.—But, sir, I know your connections and associates, and I know too, you have a saucy, lurking prejudice against your ain country:—you hate it;—yes, your mother, her family, and your brother, sir, have aw the same, dark, disaffected rankling; and, by that and their politics together, they will be the ruin of you—themselves—and of aw who connect with them.—However, nai mair of that now;—I will talk at large to you about that anon.—In the mean while, sir—notwithstanding your contempt of my advice, and your disobedience till my commands, I will convince you of my paternal attention till *your* welfare, by my management of this voluptuary—this Lord Lumbercourt,—whose daughter you are to marry. You ken, sir, that the fellow has been my patron above these five and thraty years.,

Eger. True, sir.

Sir Per. Vary weel.—And now, sir, you see, by his prodigality, he is become my dependent; and accordingly I have made my bargain with him:—the devil a baubee he has in the world but what comes thro' these clutches— for his whole estate, which has three implicit boroughs upon it,—mark—is now in my custody at nurse;—the which estate, on my paying off his debts, and allowing him a life rent of five thousand pounds per annum, is to be made over till me for my life, and at my death is to descend till ye and your issue.—The peerage of Lumbercourt, you ken, will follow of course.— So, sir, you see there are three impleecit boroughs, the whole patrimony of Lumbercourt, and a peerage at one slap.—Why it is a stroke—a hit—a hit.— —Zounds! sir, a mon may live a century and not make sic an a hit again.

Eger. It is a very advantageous bargain indeed, sir:—but what will my lord's family say to it?

Sir Per. Why, mon, he cares not if his family were aw at the devil so his luxury is but gratified:—only let him have his race-horse to feed his vanity—his harridan to drink drams with him, scrat his face, and burn his periwig, when she is in her maudlin hysterics,—and three or four discontented patriotic dependents to abuse the ministry, and settle the affairs of the nation, when they are aw intoxicated; and then, sir,:—the fellow has aw his wishes, and aw his wants—in this world—and the next.

Enter TOMLINS.

Tom. Lady Rodolpha is come, sir.

Sir Per. And my lord?

Tom. Not yet, sir,—he is about a mile behind, the servants say.

Sir Per. Let me know the instant he arrives.

Tom. I shall, sir. [*Exit.*

Sir Per. Step you out, Charles, and receive Lady Rodolpha;—and, I desire you will treat her with as much respect and gallantry as possible; for my lord has hinted that you have been very remiss as a lover.—So go, go and receive her.

Eger. I shall, sir.

Sir Per. Vary weel,—vary weel;—a guid lad: go—go and receive her as a lover should. [*Exit* Egerton.] Hah! I must keep a devilish tight hand upon this fallow, I see,—or he will be touched with the patriotic frenzy of the times, and run counter till aw my designs.—I find he has a strong inclination to have a judgment of his ain, independent of mine, in aw political matters;—but as soon as I have finally settled the marriage writings with my lord, I will have a thorough expostulation with my gentleman, I am resolved,—and fix him unalterably in his political conduct.—Ah!—I am frighted out of my wits, lest his mother's family should seduce him to desert to their party, which would totally ruin my whole scheme, and break my heart.—A fine time of day for a blockhead to turn patriot;—when the character is exploded—marked—proscribed;—why the common people—the vary vulgar—have found out the jest, and laugh at a patriot now-a-days,—-just as they do at a conjurer,—a magician,—or any other impostor in society.—

Enter TOMLINS, *and Lord* LUMBERCOURT.

Tom. Lord Lumbercourt.

Lord Lum. Sir Pertinax, I kiss your hand.

Sir Per. Your lordship's most devoted.

Lord Lum. Why, you stole a march upon me this morning;—gave me the slip, Mac;—tho' I never wanted your assistance more in my life.—I thought you would have called on me.

Sir Per. My dear lord, I beg ten millions of pardons for leaving town before you; but you ken that your lordship at dinner yesterday settled it that we should meet this morning at the levee.

Lord Lum. That I acknowledge, Mac.—I did promise to be there, I own.

Sir Per. You did, indeed.—And accordingly I was at the levee and waited there till every soul was gone, and, seeing you did not come, I concluded that your lordship was gone before.

Lord Lum. Why, to confess the truth, my dear Mac, those old sinners, Lord Freakish, General Jolly, Sir Antony Soaker, and two or three more of that set, laid hold of me last night at the opera,—and, as the General says, 'from the intelligence of my head this morning,' I believe we drank pretty deep ere we departed; ha, ha, ha!

Sir Per. Ha, ha, ha! nay, if you were with that party, my lord, I do not wonder at not seeing your lordship at the levee,

Lord Lum. The truth is, Sir Pertinax, my fellow let me sleep too long for the levee.—But I wish I had seen you before you left town—I wanted you dreadfully.

Sir Per. I am heartily sorry that I was not in the way:—but on what account did you want me?

Lord Lum. Ha, ha, ha! a cursed awkward affair.—And, ha, ha, ha! yet I cann't help laughing at it neither—tho' it vext me confoundedly.

Sir Per. Vext you, my lord! Zounds, I wish I had been with you:—but, for heaven's sake, my lord,—what was it, that could possibly vex your lordship?

Lord Lum. Why, that impudent, teasing, dunning rascal, Mahogany, my upholsterer.—You know the fellow?

Sir Per. Perfectly, my lord.

Lord Lum. The impudent scoundrel has sued me up to some damned kind of a—something or other in the law, that I think they call an execution.

Sir Per. The rascal!

Lord Lum. Upon which, sir, the fellow, by way of asking pardon—ha, ha, ha! had the modesty to wait on me two or three days ago, to inform my honour—ha, ha, ha! as he was pleased to dignify me,—that the execution was now ready to be put in force against my honour;—but that out of respect to my honour—as he had taken a great deal of my honour's money— he would not suffer his lawyer to serve it, till he had first informed my honour, because he was not willing to affront my honour; ha, ha, ha! a son of a whore!

SirPer. I never heard of so impudent a dog.

Lord Lum. Now, my dear Mac,—ha, ha, ha! as the scoundrel's apology was so very satisfactory, and his information so very agreeable—I told him that, in honour, I thought that my honour cou'd not do less than to order his honour to be paid immediately.

Sir Per. Vary weel—vary weel,—you were as complaisant as the scoundrel till the full, I think, my lord.

Lord Lum. You shall hear,—you shall hear, Mac:—so, sir, with great composure, seeing a smart oaken cudgel that stood very handily in a corner of my dressing room, I ordered two of my fellows to hold the rascal, and another to take the cudgel and return the scoundrel's civility with a good drubbing as long as the stick lasted.

Sir Per. Ha, ha, ha!—admirable!—as guid a stroke of humour as ever I heard of.—And did they drub him, my lord?

Lord Lum. Most liberally—most liberally, sir.—And there I thought the affair would have rested, till I should think proper to pay the soundrel,—but this morning, just as I was stepping into my chaise, my servants all about me, a fellow, called a tipstaff, slept up and begged the favour of my footman, who threshed the upholsterer, and of the two that held him, to go along with him upon a little business to my Lord Chief Justice.

Sir Per. The devil!

Lord Lum. And at the same instant, I, in my turn, was accosted by two other very civil scoundrels, who, with a most insolent politeness, begged my pardon, and informed me that I must not go into my own chaise.

Sir Per. How, my lord?—not into your ain carriage?

Lord Lum. No, sir: for that they, by order of the sheriff, must seize it, at the suit of a gentleman—one Mr. Mahogany, an upholsterer.

Sir Per. An impudent villain!

Lord Lum. It is all true, I assure you; so you see, my dear Mac, what a damned country this is to live in, where noblemen are obliged to pay their debts, just like merchants, coblers, peasants, or mechanics—is not that a scandal, dear Mac. to the nation?

Sir Per. My lord, it is not only a scandal, but a national grievance.

Lord Lum. Sir, there is not another nation in the world has such a grievance to complain of. Now in other countries were a mechanic to dun, and tease, and behave as this Mahogany has done,—a nobleman might extinguish the reptile in an instant; and that only at the expence of a few sequins, florins, or louis d'ors, according to the country where the affair happened.

Sir Per. Vary true, my lord, vary true—and it is monstrous that a mon of your lordship's condition is not entitled to run one of these mechanics through the body, when he is impertinent about his money; but our laws shamefully, on these occasions, make no distinction of persons amongst us.

Lord Lum. A vile policy indeed, Sir Pertinax.—But, sir, the scoundrel has seized upon the house too, that I furnished for the girl I took from the opera.

Sir Per. I never heard of sic an a scoundrel.

Lord Lum. Ay, but what concerns me most,—I am afraid, my dear Mac, that the villain will send down to Newmarket, and seize my string of horses.

Sir Per. Your string of horses? zounds! we must prevent that at all events:—that would be sic an a disgrace. I will dispatch an express to town directly to put a stop till the rascal's proceedings.

LordLum. Pr'ythee do, my dear Sir Pertinax.

Sir Per. O! it shall be done, my lord.

Lord Lum. Thou art an honest fellow, Sir Pertinax, upon honour.

Sir Per. O! my lord, it is my duty to oblige your lordship to the utmost stretch of my abeelity.

Enter TOMLINS.

Tom. Colonel Toper presents his compliments to you, sir, and having no family down with him in the country, he and Captain

Hardbottle, if not inconvenient, will do themselves the honour of taking a family dinner with you.

Sir Per. They are two of our militia officers—does your lordship know them?

LordLum. By sight only.

Sir Per. I am afraid, my lord, they will interrupt our business.

Lord Lum. Not at all: I should be glad to be acquainted with Toper; they say he's a damned jolly fellow.

Sir Per. O! devilish jolly—devilish jolly: he and the captain are the two hardest drinkers in the county.

Lord Lum. So I have heard; let us have them by all means, Mac: they will enliven the scene. How far are they from you?

Sir Per. Just across the meadows—not half a mile, my lord: a step, a step.

LordLum. O! let us have the jolly dogs, by all means.

Sir Per. My compliments—I shall be proud of their company. [*Exit* Tom.] Guif ye please, my lord, we will gang and chat a bit with the women: I have not seen Lady Rodolpha since she returned fra the Bath. I long to have a little news from her about the company there.

Lord Lum. O! she'll give you an account of them, I warrant you. [*A very loud laugh without.*

Lady Rodolpha. [*Without.*] Ha, ha, ha! weel I vow, cousin Egerton, you have a vast deal of shrewd humour.—But Lady Macsycophant, which way is Sir Pertinax?

Lady Mac. [Without._] Strait forward, madam.

Lord Lum. Here the hairbrain comes: it must be her, by the noise,

Lady Rod. [*Without.*] Allons—gude folks—follow me—sans cérémonie.

Enter Lady RODOLPHA, *Lady* MACSYCOPHANT, EGERTON, *and* SIDNEY.

Lady Rod. [*Running up to Sir* Per.] Sir Pertinax, your most devoted, most obsequious, and most obedient vassal. [*Curtsies very low.*

Sir Per. [*Bowing ridiculously low.*] Lady Rodolpha, down till the ground, my congratulations and duty attend you, and I should rejoice to kiss your ladyship's footsteps.

Lady Rod. [*Curtsying very low.*] O! Sir Pertinax, your humeelity is most sublimely complaisant:—at present, unanswerable;—but I shall intensely study to return it—fyfty fald.

Sir Per. Your ladyship does me singular honour:—weel, madam—ha! you look gaily;—weel, and how—how is your ladyship, after your jaunt till the Bath?

Lady Rod. Never better, Sir Pertinax:—as weel as youth, health, riotous spirits, and a careless happy heart can make me.

Sir Per. I am mighty glad till hear it, my lady.

Lord Lum. Ay, ay—Rodolpha is always in spirits, Sir Pertinax.—Vive la Bagatelle is the philosophy of our family,—ha? Rodolpha—ha?

Lady Rod. Traith it is, my lord; and upon honour I am determined it shall never be changed with my consent. Weel I vow—ha, ha, ha! Vive la Bagatelle would be a most brilliant motto for the chariot of a belle of fashion. What say you till my fancy, Lady Macsycophant.

Lady Mac. It would have novelty at least to recommend it, madam.

Lady Rod. Which of aw charms is the most delightful that can accompany wit, taste, love, or friendship;—for novelty I take to be the true *Je ne scais quoi* of all worldly bliss. Cousin Egerton, shou'd not you like to have a wife with Vive la Bagatelle upon her wedding chariot?

Eger. O! certainly, madam.

Lady Rod. Yes, I think it would be quite out of the common, and singularly ailegant.

Eger. Indisputably, madam:—for as a motto is a word to the wise, or rather a broad hint to the whole world of a person's taste and principles,—Vive la Bagatelle would be most expressive at first sight of your ladyship's characteristic.

Lady Rod. [*Curtsies.*] O! Maister Egerton, you touch my vary heart with your approbation—ha, ha, ha! that is the vary spirit of my intention, the instant I commence bride.—Weel! I am immensely proud that my fancy has the approbation of so sound an understanding, and so polished a taste as that of the all-accomplished [*Curtsies very low.*] Mr. Egerton.

Sir Per. Weel,—but Lady Rodolpha—I wanted to ask your ladyship some questions about the company at the Bath;—they say you had aw the world there.

Lady Rod. O, yes!—there was a vary great mob there indeed;—but vary little company.—Aw Canaille,—except our ain party.—The place was crowded with your little purse-proud mechanics;—an odd kind of queer looking animals that have started intill fortune fra lottery tickets, rich prizes at sea, gambling in Change-Alley, and sic like caprices of fortune;—and away they aw crowd to the Bath to learn genteelity, and the names, titles, intrigues, and bon-mots of us people of fashion; ha, ha, ha!

Lord Lum. Ha, ha, ha! I know them;—I know the things you mean, my dear, extremely well.—I have observed them a thousand times, and wondered where the devil they all came from; ha, ha, ha!

Lady Mac. Pray, Lady Rodolpha, what were your diversions at Bath?

Lady Rod. Guid traith, my lady, the company were my diversion,—and better na human follies ever afforded; ha, ha, ha! sic an a mixture—and sic oddities, ha, ha, ha!—a perfect Gallimaufry.—Lady Kunegunda M'Kenzie and I used to gang about till every part of this human chaos, on purpose to reconnoitre the monsters and pick up their frivolities; ha, ha, ha!

Sir Per. Ha, ha, ha! why that must have been a high entertainment till your ladyship.

Lady Rod. Superlative and inexhaustible, Sir Pertinax; ha, ha, ha!—Madam, we had in one group—a peer and a sharper,—a dutchess and a pinmaker's wife,—a boarding school miss and her grandmother,—a fat parson, a lean general, and a yellow admiral,—ha, ha, ha!—aw speaking together—and bawling and wrangling in fierce contention, as if the fame and fortune of aw the parties were to be the issue of the conflict.

Sir Per. Ha, ha, ha! pray, madam, what was the object of their contention?

Lady Rod. O! a vary important one, I assure you;—of no less consequence, madam, than how an odd trick at whist was lost, or might have been saved.

Omnes. Ha, ha, ha!

Lady Mac. Ridiculous!

Lord Lum. Ha, ha, ha! my dear Rodolpha, I have seen that very conflict a thousand times.

Sir Per. And so have I, upon honour, my lord.

Lady Rod. In another party, Sir Pertinax—ha, ha, ha! we had what was called the cabinet council, which was composed of a duke and a haberdasher,—a red hot patriot and a sneering courtier,—a discarded statesman and his scribbling chaplain,—with a busy, bawling, muckle-headed, prerogative lawyer;—all of whom were every minute ready to gang together by the lugs, about the in and the out meenistry—ha, ha, ha!

Sir Per. Ha, ha, ha! weel, that is a droll motley cabinet, I vow.—Vary whimsical upon honour.—But they are aw great politicians at Bath, and settle a meenistry there with as much ease as they do the tune of a country dance.

Lady Rod. Then, Sir Pertinax, in a retired part of the room—in a bye corner—snug—we had a Jew and a bishop—

Sir Per. A Jew and a bishop!—ha—ha—a devilish guid connection that;— and pray, my lady, what were they about?

Lady Rod. Why, sir, the bishop—was striving to convert the Jew,—while the Jew—by intervals—was slily picking up intelligence fra the bishop about the change in the meenistry, in hopes of making a stroke in the stock.

Omnes. Ha, ha, ha!

Sir Per. Ha, ha, ha! admirable! admirable! I honour the smouse:—hah! it was develish clever of him, my lord,—develish clever.

Lord Lum. Yes, yes—the fellow kept a sharp look-out.—I think it was a fair trial of skill on both sides, Mr. Egerton.

Eger. True, my lord;—but the Jew seems to have been in the fairer way to succeed.

Lord Lum. O! all to nothing, sir; ha, ha, ha!—Well, child, I like your Jew and your bishop much.—It's develish clever.—Let us have the rest of the history, pray, my dear.

Lady Rod. Guid traith, my lord, the sum total is—that there we aw danced, and wrangled, and flattered, and slandered, and gambled, and cheated, and mingled, and jumbled, and wolloped together—clean and unclean—even like the animal assembly in Noah's ark.

Omnes. Ha, ha, ha!

Lord Lum. Ha, ha, ha!—Well, you are a droll girl, Rodolpha,—and, upon my honour, ha, ha, ha!—you have given us as whimsical a sketch as ever was hit off.

Sir Per. Ah! yas, my lord, especially the animal assembly in Noah's ark.—It is an excellent picture of the oddities that one meets with at the Bath.

Lord Lum. Why yes, there is some fancy in it, I think, Egerton?

Eger. Very characteristic indeed, my lord.

Lord Lum. What say you, Mr. Sidney?

Sid. Upon my word, my lord, the lady has made me see the whole assembly in distinct colours.

Lady Rod. O! Maister Sidney, your approbation makes me as vain as a reigning toast before her looking-glass.—"But, Lady Macsycophant, I cannot help observing, that you have one uncka, unsalutary fashion here in the South, at your routs, your assemblies, and aw your dancing bouts;—the which I am astonished you do not relegate fra amongst ye.

"*Lady Mac*. Pray, madam, what may that be?

"*Lady Rod.* Why, your orgeats, capillaires, lemonades, and aw your slips and slops, with which you drench your weimbs, when you are dancing.—Upon honour, they always make a swish-swash in my bowels, and give me the wooly-wambles.

"*Omnes.* Ha, ha, ha!

"*Lord Lum.* Ho, ho, ho!—you indelicate creature,—why, my dear Rodolpha—ha, ha, ha! what are you talking about?

"*Lady Rod.* Weel, weel, my lord,—guin ye laugh till ye brust;—the fact is still true.—Now in Edinburgh—in Edinburgh, my lady—we have nai sic pinch-gut doings—for there, guid traith, we always have a guid comfortable dish of cutlets or collops, or a nice, warm, savory haggiss, with a guid swig of whiskey punch to recruit our spirits—after our dancing and sweating.

"*Omnes.* Ha, ha, ha!

"*Sir Per.* Ay, and that is much wholesomer, Lady Rodolpha, than aw their slips and their slops here in the south.

"*Lord Lum.* Ha, ha, ha! Well, my dear Rodolpha, you are a droll girl, upon honour,—and very entertaining, I vow; [*He whispers.*]—but, my dear child,—a little too much upon the dancing, and sweating, and the wolly-wambles.

"*Omnes.* Ha, ha, ha!"

Enter TOMLINS.

Tom. Colonel Toper and Captain Hardbottle are come, sir.

Sir Per. O! vary weel.—Dinner directly.

Tom. It is ready, sir. [*Exit.*

Sir Per. My lord, we attend your lordship.

Lord Lum. Lady Mac, your ladyship's hand, if you please. [*Exit with Lady* Macsycophant.

Sir Per. And here, Lady Rodolpha, is an Arcadian swain that has a hand at your ladyship's devotion.

Lady Rod. [*Giving her hand to* Egerton.] And I, sir, have one at his.— There, sir:—as to hearts, ye ken, cousin, they are not brought into the account of human dealings now-a-days.

Eger. O! madam, they are mere temporary baubles, especially in courtship; and no more to be depended upon than the weather, or a lottery ticket.

Lady Rod, Ha, ha, ha! twa excellent similes, I vow, Mr. Egerton.—Excellent! for they illustrate the vagaries and inconstancy of my dissipated heart as exactly as if you had meant to describe it. [*Exit with* Eger.

Sir Per. Ha, ha, ha! what a vast fund of spirits and guid humour she has, Maister Sidney.

Sid. A great fund indeed, Sir Pertinax.

Sir Per. Come, let us till dinner.—Hah! by this time to-morrow, Maister Sidney, I hope we shall have every thing ready for you to put the last hand till the happiness of your friend and pupil;—and then, sir—my cares will be over for this life:—for as to my other son, I expect nai guid of him, nor shou'd I grieve, were I to see him in his coffin.—But this match,—O! it will make me the happiest of aw human beings. [*Exeunt.*

END OF THE SECOND ACT.

ACT III. SCENE I.

Enter Sir PERTINAX *and* EGERTON.

Sir Per. [*In warm resentment.*] Zoons! sir, I wull not hear a word about it:—I insist upon it you are wrong:—you shou'd have paid your court till my lord, and not have scrupled swallowing a bumper or twa, or twenty, till oblige him.

Eger. Sir, I did drink his toast in a bumper.

Sir Per. Yes—you did;—but how? how?—just as a bairn takes physic— with aversions and wry faces, which my lord observed: then, to mend the matter, the moment that he and the colonel got intill a drunken dispute about religion, you slily slunged away.

Eger. I thought, sir, it was time to go, when my lord insisted upon half pint bumpers.

Sir Per. Sir, that was not levelled at you, but at the colonel, in order to try his bottom; but they aw agreed that you and I should drink out of smaw glasses.

Eger. But, sir, I beg pardon:—I did not choose to drink any more.

Sir Per. But zoons! sir, I tell you there was a necessity for your drinking more.

Eger. A necessity! in what respect, pray, sir?

Sir Per. Why, sir, I have a certain point to carry, independent of the lawyers, with my lord, in this agreement of your marriage—about which I am afraid we shall have a warm squabble—and therefore I wanted your assistance in it.

Eger. But how, sir, could my drinking contribute to assist you in your squabble?

Sir Per. Yes, sir, it would have contributed—and greatly have contributed to assist me.

Eger. How so, sir?

Sir Per. Nay, sir, it might have prevented the squabble entirely; for as my lord is proud of you for a son-in-law, and is fond of your little French songs, your stories, and your bon-mots, when you are in the humour,—and guin you had but staid—and been a little jolly—and drank half a score bumpers with him, till he got a little tipsy—I am sure, when we had him in that mood, we might have settled the point as I could wish it, among ourselves, before the lawyers came: but now, sir, I do not ken what will be the consequence.

Eger. But when a man is intoxicated, would that have been a seasonable time to settle business, sir?

Sir Per. The most seasonable, sir:—for, sir, when my lord is in his cups—his suspicion is asleep—and his heart is aw jollity, fun, and guid fellowship; and sir, can there be a happier moment than that for a bargain, or to settle a dispute with a friend? What is it you shrug up your shoulders at, sir?

Eger. At my own ignorance, sir;—for I understand neither the philosophy nor the morality of your doctrine.

Sir Per. I know you do not, sir,—and, what is worse—you never wull, understand it, as you proceed: in one word, Charles, I have often told you, and now again I tell you, once for aw, that the manoeuvres of pliability are as necessary to rise in the world, as wrangling and logical subtlety are to rise at the bar: why you see, sir, I have acquired a noble fortune, a princely fortune—and how do you think I raised it?

Eger. Doubtless, sir, by your abilities.

Sir Per. Doubtless, sir, you are a blockhead:—nai, sir, I'll tell you how I raised it. Sir, I raised it—by bowing; [*Bows ridiculously low.*] by bowing: sir, I never could stand straight in the presence of a great man, but always bowed, and bowed, and bowed—as it were by instinct.

Eger. How do you mean by instinct, sir?

Sir Per. How do I mean by instinct? why, sir, I mean by—by—by the instinct of interest, sir, which is the universal instinct of mankind. Sir, it is wonderful to think, what a cordial, what an amicable, nay, what an infallible influence, bowing has upon the pride and vanity of human nature. Charles, answer me sincerely, have you a mind to be convinced of the force of my doctrine, by example and demonstration?

Eger. Certainly, sir.

Sir Per. Then, sir, as the greatest favour I can confer upon you, I'll give you a short sketch of the stages of my bowing,—as an excitement, and a landmark for you to bow be—and as an infallible nostrum to rise in the world.

Eger. Sir, I shall be proud to profit by your experience.

Sir Per. Vary weel, sir: sit ye down then, sit you down here: *[They sit down.]*—and now, sir, you must recall to your thoughts, that your grandfather was a man, whose penurious income of half pay was the sum total of his fortune;—and, sir, aw my provision fra him was a modicum of Latin, an expertness in arithmetic, and a short system of worldly counsel; the principal ingredients of which were, a persevering industry, a rigid economy, a smooth tongue, a pliability of temper, and a constant attention to make every man well pleased with himself.

Eger. Very prudent advice, sir.

Sir Per. Therefore, sir, I lay it before you.—Now, sir, with these materials I set out a raw-boned stripling fra the north, to try my fortune with them here in the south; and my first step intill the world was, a beggarly clerkship in Sawney Gordon's counting house, here in the city of London, which you'll say afforded but a barren sort of a prospect.

Eger. It was not a very fertile one indeed, sir.

Sir Per. The reverse, the reverse: weel, sir, seeing myself in this unprofitable situation, I reflected deeply; I cast about my thoughts morning, noon, and night, and markt every man and every mode of prosperity,—at last I concluded that a matrimonial adventure, prudently conducted, would be the readiest gait I could gang for the bettering of my condition, and accordingly I set about it: now, sir, in this pursuit, beauty! beauty!—ah! beauty often struck mine een, and played about my heart! and fluttered, and beat, and knocked, and knocked, but the devil an entrance I ever let it get;—for I observed, sir, that beauty—is generally—a proud, vain, saucy, expensive, impertinent sort of a commodity.

Eger. Very justly observed, sir.

Sir Per. And therefore, sir, I left it to prodigals and coxcombs, that could afford to pay for it; and in its stead, sir, mark! I looked out for an ancient, weel-jointured, superannuated dowager:—a consumptive, toothless, ptisicky, wealthy widow,—or a shrivelled, cadaverous piece of deformity in the shape of an izzard, or a appersi-and,—or, in short, ainy thing, ainy thing that had the siller, the siller,—for that, sir, was the north star of my affections. Do you take me, sir; was nai that right?

Eger. O! doubtless—doubtless, sir.

Sir Per. Now, sir, where do you think I ganged to look for this woman with the siller?—nai till court, nai till playhouses or assemblies—nai, sir. I ganged till the kirk, till the anabaptist, independent, bradlonian, and muggletonian meetings; till the morning and evening service of churches and chapels of ease, and till the midnight, melting, conciliating love-feasts of the methodists; and there, sir, at last, I fell upon an old, slighted, antiquated, musty maiden, that looked—ha, ha, ha! she looked just like a skeleton in a surgeon's glass case. Now, sir, this miserable object was religiously angry with herself and aw the world; had nai comfort but in metaphysical visions, and supernatural deliriums; ha, ha, ha! Sir, she was as mad—as mad as a Bedlamite.

Eger. Not improbable, sir, there are numbers of poor creatures in the same condition.

Sir Per. O! numbers—numbers. Now, sir, this cracked creature used to pray, and sing, and sigh, and groan, and weep, and wail, and gnash her teeth constantly, morning and evening, at the Tabernacle in Moorfields: and as soon as I found she had the siller, aha! guid traith, I plumpt me down upon my knees, close by her—cheek by jowl—and prayed, and sighed, and sung, and groaned, and gnashed my teeth as vehemently as she could do for the life of her; ay, and turned up the whites of mine een, till the strings awmost crackt again:—I watcht her motions, handed her till her chair, waited on her home, got most religiously intimate with her in a week,—married her in a fortnight, buried her in a month;—touched the siller, and with a deep suit of mourning, a melancholy port, a sorrowful visage, and a joyful heart, I began the world again;—and this, sir, was the first bow, that is, the first effectual bow, I ever made till the vanity of human nature:—now, sir, do you understand this doctrine?

Eger. Perfectly well, sir.

Sir Per. Ay, but was it not right? was it not ingenious, and weel hit off?

Eger. Certainly, sir: extremely well.

Sir Per. My next bow, sir, was till your ain mother, whom I ran away with fra the boarding school; by the interest of whose family I got a guid smart place in the Treasury:—and, sir, my vary next step was intill Parliament; the which I entered with as ardent and as determined an ambition as ever agitated the heart of Cæsar himself. Sir, I bowed, and watched, and hearkened, and ran about, backwards and forwards; and attended, and dangled upon the then great man, till I got intill the vary bowels of his confidence,—and then, sir, I wriggled, and wrought, and wriggled, till I wriggled myself among the very thick of them: hah! I got my snack of the clothing, the foraging, the contracts, the lottery tickets—and aw the political bonusses;—till at length, sir, I became a much wealthier man than one half of the golden calves I had been so long a bowing to: [*He rises, and* Eger. *rises too.*]—and was nai that bowing to some purpose?

Eger. It was indeed, sir.

Sir Per. But are you convinced of the guid effects, and of the utility of bowing?

Eger. Thoroughly, sir.

Sir Per. Sir, it is infallible:—but, Charles, ah! while I was thus bowing, and wriggling, and raising this princely fortune,—ah! I met with many heart-sores and disappointments fra the want of literature, eloquence, and other popular abeleties. Sir, guin I could but have spoken in the house, I should have done the deed in half the time; but the instant I opened my mouth there, they aw fell a laughing at me;—aw which deficiencies, sir, I determined, at any expence, to have supplied by the polished education of a son, who, I hoped, would one day raise the house of Macsycophant till the highest pitch of ministerial ambition. This, sir, is my plan: I have done my part of it; Nature has done hers: you are popular, you are eloquent; aw parties like and respect you; and now, sir, it only remains for you to be directed—completion follows.

Eger. Your liberality, sir, in my education, and the judicious choice you made of the worthy gentleman, to whose virtue and abilities you entrusted me, are obligations I shall ever remember with the deepest filial gratitude.

Sir Per. Vary weel, sir: but, Charles, have you had any conversation yet with Lady Rodolpha, about the day of your marriage—your liveries—your equipage—or your domestic establishment?

Eger. Not yet, sir.

Sir Per. Poh! why there again now you are wrong—vary wrong.

Eger. Sir, we have not had an opportunity.

Sir Per. Why, Charles, you are vary tardy in this business.

Lord Lum. [*Sings without, flusht with wine.*] 'What have we with day to do?'

Sir Per. O! here comes my lord.

Lord Lum. 'Sons of care, 'twas made for you,' [*Enters, drinking a dish of coffee*: TOMLINS *waiting with a salver in his hand.*] —'Sons of care, 'twas made for you.' Very, good coffee indeed, Mr. Tomlins. 'Sons of care, 'twas made for you.' Here, Mr. Tomlins.

Tom. Will your lordship please to have another dish?

Lord Lum. No more, Mr. Tomlins. [*Exit* Tomlins.] Ha, ha, ha! my host of the Scotch pints, we have had warm work.

Sir Per. Yes; you pushed the bottle about, my lord, with the joy and vigour of a Bacchanal.

Lord Lum. That I did, my dear Mac; no loss of time with me: I have but three motions, old boy,—charge—toast—fire—and off we go: ha, ha, ha! that's my exercise.

Sir Per. And fine warm exercise it is, my lord,—especially with the half-pint glasses.

Lord Lum. Zounds! it does execution point blanc:—ay, ay, none of your pimping acorn glasses for me, but your manly, old English half-pint bumpers, my dear: they try a fellow's stamina at once:—but, where's Egerton?

Sir Per. Just at hand, my lord; there he stands—looking at your lordship's picture.

Lord Lum. My dear Egerton.

Eger. Your lordship's most obedient.

Lord Lum. I beg pardon: I did not see you: I am sorry you left us so soon after dinner: had you staid, you would have been highly entertained. I have made such examples of the commissioner, the captain, and the colonel.

Eger. So I understand, my lord.

Lord Lum. But, Egerton, I have slipt from the company for a few moments, on purpose to have a little chat with you. Rodolpha tells me she fancies there is a kind of demur on your side, about your marriage with her.

Sir Per. A demur! how so, my lord?

Lord Lum. Why, as I was drinking my coffee with the women just now, I desired they would fix the wedding night, and the etiquette of the ceremony; upon which the girl burst into a loud laugh, telling me she supposed I was joking, for that Mr. Egerton had never yet given her a single glance or hint upon the subject.

Sir Per. My lord, I have been just now talking to him about his shyness to the lady.

Enter TOMLINS..

Tom. Counsellor Plausible is come, sir, and serjeant Eitherside.

Sir Per. Why then we can settle the business this very evening, my lord.

Lord Lum. As well as in seven years: and, to make the way as short as possible, pray, Mr. Tomlins, present your master's compliments and mine to Lady Rodolpha, and let her ladyship know we wish to speak with her directly: [*Exit* Tomlins.]—He shall attack her this instant, Sir Pertinax.

Sir Per. Ay! this is doing business effectually, my lord.

Lord Lum. O! I will pit them in a moment, Sir Pertinax,—that will bring them into the heat of the action at once, and save a great deal of awkwardness on both sides. O! here your dulcinea comes, sir.

Enter Lady RODOLPHA, *singing, a music paper in her hand.*

Lady Rod. I have been learning this air of Constantia: I protest, her touch on the harpsichord is quite brilliant, and really her voice not amiss. Weel, Sir Pertinax, I attend your commands, and yours, my paternal lord. [*Lady* Rod. *curtsies very low; my lord bows very low, and answers in the same tone and manner.*]

Lord Lum. Why, then, my filial lady, we are to inform you that the commission for your ladyship and this enamoured cavalier, commanding you to serve your country, jointly and inseparably, in the honourable and forlorn hope of matrimony, is to be signed this very evening.

Lady Rod. This evening, my lord!

Lord Lum. This evening, my lady. Come, Sir Pertinax, let us leave them to settle their liveries, wedding-suits, carriages, and all their amorous equipage, for the nuptial campaign.

Sir Per. Ha, ha, ha! excellent! excellent! weel, I vow, my lord, you are a great officer:—this is as guid a manoeuvre to bring on a rapid engagement as the ablest general of them aw could have started.

Lord Lum. Ay, ay! leave them together; they'll soon come to a right understanding, I warrant you, or the needle and loadstone have lost their sympathy. [*Exit Lord* Lum. *and Sir* Per.

[*Lady* Rodolpha *stands at that side of the Stage, where they went off, in amazement:* Egerton *is at the opposite side, who, after some anxious emo-*

tion, settles into a deep reflection: – this part of the scene must be managed by a nice whispering tone of self-conversation mutually observed by the Lovers.]

Lady Rod. [*Aside.*] Why, this is downright tyranny! it has quite dampt my spirits; and my betrothed, yonder, seems planet-struck too, I think.

Eger. [*Aside.*] A whimsical situation, mine!

Lady Rod. [*Aside.*] Ha, ha, ha! methinks we look like a couple of cautious generals, that are obliged to take the field, but neither of us seems willing to come till action.

Eger. [*Aside.*] I protest, I know not how to address her.

Lady Rod. [*Aside.*] He will nai advance, I see: what am I to do in this affair? guid traith, I will even do, as I suppose many brave heroes have done before me, – clap a guid face upon the matter, and so conceal an aching heart under a swaggering countenance. [*As she advances, she points at him, and smothers a laugh; but when she speaks to him, the tone must be* loud, *and rude on the word* Sir.] *Sir,* as we have, – by the commands of our guid fathers, a business of some little consequence to transact, – I hope you will excuse my taking the liberty of recommending a chair till you, for the repose of your body – in the embarrassed deliberation of your perturbed spirits.

Eger. [*Greatly embarrassed.*] Madam, I beg your pardon. [*Hands her a chair, then one for himself.*] Please to sit, madam. [*They sit down with great ceremony: she sits down first. He sits at a distance from her. They are silent for some time. He coughs, hems, and adjusts himself. She mimicks him.*]

Lady Rod. [*Aside.*] Aha! he's resolved not to come too near till me, I think.

Eger. [*Aside.*] A pleasant interview, this – hem, hem!

Lady Rod. [*Aside, mimicks him to herself.*] Hem! he will not open the congress, I see. – Then I will. – [*very loud.*] *Come, sir,* when will you begin?

Eger. [*Greatly surprised.*] Begin! what, madam?

Lady Rod. To make love till me.

Eger. Love, madam!

Lady Rod. Ay, love, sir.—Why, you have never said a word till me on the subject,—nor cast a single glance at me,—nor heaved one tender sigh,—nor even secretly squeezed my loof:—now, sir, thof our fathers are so tyrannical as to dispose of us without the consent of our hearts;—yet you, sir, I hope, have more humanity than to think of marrying me without administering some of the preliminaries, usual on those occasions:—if not till my understanding and sentiments, yet till the vanity of my sex, at least, I hope you will pay some little tribute of ceremony and adulation: that, I think, I have a right to expect.

Eger. Madam, I own your reproach is just:—I shall therefore no longer disguise my sentiments, but fairly let you know my heart.

Lady Rod. [*Starts up, and runs to him.*] That's right,—that is right, cousin;—honourably and affectionately right;—that is what I like of aw things in my swain.—Ay, ay, cousin—open your mind frankly till me, as a true lover shou'd.—But sit you down—sit you down again: I shall return your frankness and your passion, cousin, with a melting tenderness, equal till the amorous enthusiasm of an ancient heroine.

Eger. Madam, if you will hear me——

Lady Rod. But, remember, you must begin with fervency,—and a most rapturous vehemency:—for you are to consider, cousin, that our match is nai to arise fra the union of hearts, and a long decorum of ceremonious courtship;—but is instantly to start at once—out of necessity, or mere accident;—ha, ha, ha! like a match in an ancient romance,—where you ken, cousin,—the knight and the damsel are mutually smitten and dying for each other at first sight,—or by an amorous sympathy before they exchange a single glance.

Eger. Dear madam, you entirely mistake——

Lady Rod. And our fathers,—ha, ha, ha! our fathers are to be the dark magicians that are to fascinate our hearts and conjure us together, whether we will or not.

Eger. Ridiculous!

Lady Rod. So now, cousin, with the true romantic enthusiasm,—you are to suppose me the lady of the enchanted castle, and you—ha, ha, ha! you are to be the knight of the sorrowful countenance—ha, ha, ha! and, upon honour—you look the character admirably;—ha, ha, ha!

Eger. Rude trifling creature!

Lady Rod. Come, sir,—why do you nai begin to ravish me with your valour, your vows, your knight errantry, and your amorous phrenzy.—Nay, nay, nay! guin you do nai begin at once, the lady of the enchanted castle will vanish in a twinkling.

Eger. Lady Rodolpha, I know your talent for raillery well;—but at present, in my case, there is a kind of cruelty in it.

Lady Rod. Raillery! upon honour, cousin, you mistake me quite and clean.—I am serious—very serious;—ay, and I have cause to be serious;— nay, I will submit my case even till yourself. [*Whines*.] Can any poor lassy be in a more lamentable condition, than to be sent four hundred miles, by the command of a positive grandmother, to marry a man, who I find has no more affection for me,—than if I had been his wife these seven years.

Eger. Madam, I am extremely sorry— —

Lady Rod. [*Cries and sobs*.] But it is vary weel, cousin.—I see your unkindness and aversion plain enough,—and, sir, I must tell you fairly, you are the ainly man that ever slighted my person,—or that drew tears fra these een.—But—it is vary weel—it's vary weel—I will return till Scotland to-morrow morning, and let my grandmother know how I have been affronted by your slights, your contempts, and your aversions.

Eger. If you are serious, madam, your distress gives me a deep concern;—but affection is not in our power; and when you know that my heart is irrecoverably given to another woman, I think, your understanding and good nature will not only pardon my past coldness and neglect of you,—but forgive me when I tell you, I never can have that honour which is intended me,—by a connection with your ladyship.

Lady Rod. [*Starting up*.] How, sir!—are you serious?

Eger. [*Rises*.] Madam, I am too deeply interested, both as a man of honour and a lover, to act otherwise with you on so tender a subject.

Lady Rod. And so you persist in slighting me?

Eger. I beg your pardon, madam; but I must be explicit, and at once declare—that I never can give my hand where I cannot give my heart.

Lady Rod. [*In great anger*.] Why then, sir, I must tell you, that your declaration is sic an affront as nai woman of spirit can, or ought to bear:—and here I make a solemn vow, never to pardon it, but on one condition.

Eger. If that condition be in my power, madam——

Lady Rod. [*Snaps him up*.] Sir, it is in your power.

Eger. Then, madam, you may command me.

Lady Rod. [*With a firm peremptory command*]. Why then, sir, the condition is this;—you must here give me your honour,—that nai importunity,—command,—or menace of your father,—in fine, that nai consideration whatever,—shall induce you to take me, Rodolpha Lumbercourt, to be your wedded wife.

Eger. Madam, I most solemnly promise, I never will.

Lady Rod. And I, sir, most solemnly, and sincerely [*Curtsies*.] thank you—for [*Curtsies*.] your resolution, and your agreeable aversion—ha, ha, ha! for you have made me as happy as a poor wretch, reprieved in the vary instant of intended execution.

Eger. Pray, madam, how am I to understand all this?

Lady Rod.[*With frankness, and, a reverse of manners*.] Why, sir, your frankness and sincerity demand the same behaviour on my side;—therefore, without farther disguise or ambiguity, know, sir, that I myself [*With a deep sigh*.] am as deeply smitten with a certain swain, as I understand you are with your Constantia.

Eger. Indeed, madam!

Lady Rod. [*With an amiable, soft, tender sincerity*.] O! sir, notwithstanding aw my shew of courage and mirth,—here I stand—as errant a trembling Thisbe, as ever sighed or mourned for her Pyramus,—and, sir, aw my extravagant levity and ridiculous behaviour in your presence now, and ever since *your* father prevailed upon *mine* to consent till this match, has been a premeditated scheme to provoke your gravity and guid sense intill a cordial disgust, and a positive refusal.

Eger. Madam, you have contrived and executed your scheme most happily.

Lady Rod. Then, since Cupid has thus luckily disposed of you till your Constantia, and me till my swain, we have nothing to think of now, sir, but to contrive how to reduce the inordinate passions of our parents intill a temper of prudence and humanity.

Eger. Most willingly I consent to your proposal.— —But, with your leave, madam, if I may presume so far;—'pray, who is your lover?

Lady Rod. Why, in that too I shall surprise you perhaps more than ever.—In the first place—he is a beggar—and in disgrace with an unforgiving father;—and in the next place,—he is [*Curtsies.*] your ain brother.

Eger. Is it possible?

Lady Rod. A most amorous truth, sir;—that is, as far as a woman can answer for her ain heart. [*in a laughing gaiety.*] So you see, cousin Charles, thof I you'd nai mingle affections with *you*—I have nai ganged out of the family.

Eger. [*A polite rapture, frank.*] Madam, give me leave to congratulate myself upon your affection,—you cou'd not have placed it on a worthier object; and, whatever is to be our chance in this lottery of our parents, be assured that my fortune shall be devoted to your happiness and his.

Lady Rod. Generous, indeed, cousin—but not a whit nobler, I assure you, than your brother Sandy believes of you.—And, be assured, sir, that we shall both remember it, while the heart feels, or the memory retains a sense of gratitude.—But now, sir, let me ask one question:—Pray, how is your mother affected in this business?

Eger. She knows of my passion, and will, I am sure, be a friend to the common cause.

Lady Rod. Ah! that's lucky. Our first step then must be to take her advice upon our conduct, so as to keep our fathers in the dark till we can hit off some measure that will wind them about till our ain purpose, and the common interest of our ain passion.

Eger. You are very right, madam, for, should my father suspect my brother's affection for your ladyship, or mine for Constantia, there is no guessing what wou'd be the consequence.—His whole happiness depends upon this bargain with my lord; for it gives him the possession of three boroughs, and those, madam, are much dearer to him than the happiness of his children. I am sorry to say it, but, to gratify his political rage, he wou'd sacrifice every social tie, that is dear to friend or family. [*Exeunt.*

END OF THE THIRD ACT.

ACT IV. SCENE I.

Enter Sir PERTINAX, *and Counsellor* PLAUSIBLE.

Sir Per. No, no.—Come away, Counsellor Plausible;—come away, I say;—let them chew upon it.—Why, counsellor, did you ever see so impertinent, so meddling, and so obstinate a blockhead, as that Serjeant Eitherside? Confound the fellow—he has put me out of aw temper.

Plaus. He is very positive, indeed, Sir Pertinax,—and no doubt was intemperate and rude. But, Sir Pertinax, I wou'd not break off the match notwithstanding; for certainly, even without the boroughs, it is an advantageous bargain both to you and your son.

Sir Per. But, zounds! Plausible, do you think I will give up the nomination till three boroughs?—Why I wou'd rather give him twenty, nay thirty thousand pounds in any other part of the bargain:—especially at this juncture, when votes are likely to become so valuable.—Why, man, if a certain affair comes on, they will rise above five hundred per cent.

Plaus. You judge very rightly, Sir Pertinax;—but what shall we do in this case? for Mr. Serjeant insists that you positively agreed to my lord's having the nomination to the three boroughs during his own life.

Sir Per. Why yes,—in the first sketch of the agreement, I believe I did consent:—but at that time, man, my lord's affairs did not appear to be half so desperate, as I now find they turn out.—Sir, he must acquiesce in whatever I demand, for I have got him intill sic an a hobble that he cannot— —

Plaus. No doubt, Sir Pertinax, you have him absolutely in your power.

Sir Per. Vary weel:—And ought rial a man to make his vantage of it?

Plaus. No doubt you ought;—no manner of doubt.—But, Sir Pertinax, there is a secret spring in this business, that you do not seem to perceive;—and which, I am afraid, governs the matter respecting these boroughs.

Sir Per. What spring do you mean, counsellor?

Plaus. Why this Serjeant Eitherside,—I have some reason to think that my lord is tied down by some means or other to bring the serjeant in, the very first vacancy, for one of these boroughs;—now that, I believe, is the sole motive why the serjeant is so strenuous that my lord should keep the boroughs in his own power;—fearing that you might reject him for some man of your own.

Sir Per. Odswunds and death! Plausible, you are clever,—devilish clever.—By the blood, you have hit upon the vary string that has made aw thjs discord.—Oh! I see it,—I see it now.—But hauld—hauld—bide a wee bit—a wee bit, man;—I have a thought come intill my head—yes—I think, Plausible, that with a little twist in our negotiation that this vary string, properly tuned, may be still made to produce the vary harmony we wish for.—Yes, yes! I have it: this serjeant, I see, understands business—and, if I am not. mistaken, knows how to take a hint.

Plaus. O! nobody better, Sir Pertinax.

Sir Per. Why then, Plausible, the short road is always the best with sic a man.—You. must even come up till his mark at once, and assure him from me—that I will secure him a seat for one of these vary boroughs.

Plaus. O! that will do, Sir Pertinax—that will do, I'll answer for't.

Sir Per. And further—I beg you will let him know that I think myself obliged to consider him in this affair, as acting for me as weel as for my lord,—as a common friend till baith:—and for the services he has already done us, make my special compliments till him—and pray let this amicable bit of paper be my faithful advocate to convince him of what my gratitude further intends for his great [*Gives him a bank-bill.*] equity in adjusting this agreement betwixt my lord and me.

Plaus. Ha, ha, ha!—upon my word, Sir Pertinax, this is noble.—Ay, ay! this is an eloquent bit of paper indeed.

Sir Per. Maister Plausible, in aw human dealings the most effectual method is that of ganging at once till the vary bottom of a man's heart:—for if we expect that men shou'd serve us,—we must first win their affections by serving them.—O! here they baith come.

Enter Lord LUMBERCOURT, *and Serjeant* EITHERSIDE.

Lord Lum. My dear Sir Pertinax, what could provoke you to break off this business so abruptly? you are really wrong in the point,—and if you will give yourself time to recollect, you will find that my having the nomination to the boroughs for my life was a preliminary article;—I appeal to Mr. Serjeant Eitherside here, whether I did not always understand it so.

_Serj._I assure you, Sir Pertinax, that in all his lordship's conversation with me upon this business, and in his positive instructions,—both he and I always understood the nomination to be in my lord, durantê vitâ.

SirPer. Why, then my lord, to shorten the dispute, aw that I can say in answer till your lordship is—that there has been a total mistake betwixt us in that point,—and therefore the treaty must end here. I give it up.— O! I wash my hands of it for ever.

Plaus. Well, but gentlemen, gentlemen, a little patience.—Sure this mistake, some how or other, may be rectified.—Pr'ythee, Mr. Serjeant, let you and I step into the next room by ourselves, and reconsider the clause relative to the boroughs, and try if we cannot hit upon a medium that will be agreeable to both parties.

Serj. [*With great warmth.*] Mr. Plausible, I have considered the clause fully;—am entirely master of the question;—my lord cannot give up the point.—It is unkind and unreasonable to expect it.

Plaus. Nay, Mr. Serjeant, I beg you will not misunderstand me. Do not think I want his lordship to give up any point without an equivalent.—Sir Pertinax, will you permit Mr. Serjeant and me to retire a few moments to reconsider this point?

Sir Per. With aw my heart, Maister Plausible; any thing to oblige his lordship—any thing to accomodate his lordship—any thing.

Plaus. What say you, my lord?

Lord Lum Nay, I submit it entirely to you and Mr. Serjeant.

Plaus. Come, Mr. Serjeant, let us retire.

Lord Lum. Ay, ay,—go, Mr. Serjeant, and hear what Mr. Plausible has to say.

Serj. Nay, I'll wait on Mr. Plausible, my lord, with all my heart; but I am sure I cannot suggest the shadow of a reason for altering my present opinion: impossible—impossible.

Plaus. Well, well, Mr. Serjeant, do not be positive. I am sure, reason, and your client's conveniency, will always make you alter your opinion.

Serj. Ay, ay—reason, and my client's conveniency, Mr. Plausible, will always controul my opinion, depend upon it: ay, ay! there you are right. Sir, I attend you. [*Exeunt Lawyers.*

Sir Per. I am sorry, my lord, extremely sorry indeed, that this mistake has happened.

Lord Lum. Upon my honour, and so am I, Sir Pertinax.

Sir Per. But come now, after aw, your lordship must allow you have been in the wrong: come, my dear lord, you must allow me that now.

Lord Lum. How so, my dear Sir Pertinax?

Sir Per. Not about the boroughs, my lord, for those I do no mind of a bawbee;—but about your distrust of my friendship.—Why, do you think now—I appeal till your ain breast, my lord—do you think, I say, that I should ever have slighted your lordship's nomination till these boroughs.

Lord Lum. Why, really, I do not think you would, Sir Pertinax, but one must be directed by one's lawyer, you know.

Sir Per. Hah! my lord, lawyers are a dangerous species of animals to have any dependance upon: they are always starting punctilios and difficulties among friends. Why, my dear lord, it is their interest that aw mankind should be at variance: for disagreement is the vary manure with which they enrich and fatten the land of litigation; and as they find that that constantly promotes the best crop, depend upon it, they will always be sure to lay it on as thick as they can.

Lord Lum. Come, come, my dear Sir Pertinax, you must not be angry with the serjeant for his insisting so warmly on this point—for those boroughs, you know, are my sheet anchor.

Sir Per. I know it, my lord,—and, as an instance of my promptness to study, and of my acquiescence till your lordship's inclination, as I see that this Serjeant Eitherside wishes you weel and you him, I think now he would be as guid a man to be returned for one of those boroughs as could be pitched upon—and as such, I humbly recommend him till your lordship's consideration.

Lord Lum. Why, my dear Sir Pertinax, to tell you the truth, I have already promised him. He must be in for one of them, and that is one reason why I insisted so strenuously: he must be in.

Sir Per. And why not? odswunds! why not? is nai your word a fiat? and will it nai be always so till me? are ye nai my friend—my patron—and are we nai, by this match of our children, to be united intill one interest?

Lord Lum. So I understand it, I own, Sir Pertinax.

Sir Per. My lord, it can nai be otherwise: then, for Heaven's sake, as your lordship and I can have but one interest for the future, let us have nai mair words about these paltry boroughs, but conclude the agreement just as it stands; otherwise there must be new writings drawn, new consultations of lawyers, new objections and delays will arise,—creditors will be impatient and impertinent, so that we shall nai finish the Lord knows when.

Lord Lum. You are right, you are right: say no more, Mac, say no more. Split the lawyers—you judge the point better than all Westminster-hall could. It shall stand as it is: yes, you shall settle it your own way: for your interest and mine are the same, I see plainly.

Sir Per. No doubt of it, my lord.

Lord Lum. O! here the lawyers come.

Enter Counsellor PLAUSIBLE *and Serjeant* EITHERSIDE.

Lord Lum. So, gentlemen—well, what have you done? how are your opinions now?

Serj. My lord, Mr. Plausible has convinced me—fully convinced me.

Plaus. Yes, my lord, I have convinced him; I have laid such arguments before Mr. Serjeant as were irresistible.

Serj. He has indeed, my lord: besides, as Sir Pertinax gives his honour that your lordship's nomination shall be sacredly observed, why, upon a nearer review of the whole matter, I think it will be the wiser measure to conclude the agreement just as it is drawn.

Lord Lum. I am very glad you think so, Mr. Serjeant, because that is my opinion too: so, my dear Eitherside, do you and Plausible dispatch the business now as soon as possible.

Serj. My lord, every thing will be ready in less than an hour. Come, Mr. Plausible, let us go and fill up the blanks, and put the last hand to the writings on our part.

Plaus. I attend you, Mr. Serjeant. [*Exeunt Lawyers*.

Lord Lum. And while the lawyers are preparing the writings, Sir Pertinax, I will go and saunter with the women.

Sir Per. Do, do, my lord: and I will come till you presently.

Lord Lum. Very well, my dear Mac, I shall expect you. [*Exit singing, 'Sons of care,' &c.*

Sir Per. So! a little flattery mixt with the finesse of a gilded promise on one side, and a quantum sufficit of the aurum palpabile on the other, have at last made me the happiest father in Great-Britain. Hah! my heart expands itself, as it were thro' every part of my whole body, at the completion of this business, and feels nothing but dignity and elevation.—Hauld! hauld! bide a wee! bide a wee! I have but one little matter mair in this affair to adjust, and then, Sir Pertinax, you may dictate till Fortune herself, and send her to govern fools, while you shew and convince the world that wise men always govern her. Wha's there? [*Enter Footman*.]—Tell my son Egerton, I would speak with him here in the library. [*Exit Footman*]—Now I have settled the grand point with my lord, this, I think, is the proper juncture to feel the political pulse of my spark, and, once for aw, to set it to the exact measure that I would have it constantly beat. [*Enter* Egerton.]—Come hither, Charles.

Eger. Your pleasure, sir.

Sir Per. About twa hours since I told you, Charles, that I received this letter express, complaining of your brother's activity at an election in Scotland against a particular friend of mine, which has given great offence; and, sir, you are mentioned in the letter as weel as he: to be plain, I must roundly tell you, that on this interview depends my happiness as a father and as a man; and my affection to you, sir, as a son for the remainder of our days.

Eger. I hope, sir, I shall never do any thing either to forfeit your affection, or disturb your happiness.

Sir Per. I hope so too—but to the point.—The fact is this: there has been a motion made this vary day to bring on the grand affair—which is settled for Friday seven-night:—now, sir, as you are popular—have talents, and are weel heard, it is expected, and I insist upon it, that you endeavour to atone, sir, for your late misconduct, by preparing, and taking a large share in that question, and supporting it with aw your power.

Eger, Sir, I have always divided as you directed, except on one occasion; never voted against your friends, only in that affair.—But, sir, I hope you will not so exert your influence as to insist upon my supporting a measure by an obvious, prostituted sophistry, in direct opposition to my character and my conscience.

Sir Per. Conscience! why, you are mad! did you ever hear any man talk of conscience in political matters? Conscience, quotha? I have been in Parliament these three and thraty years, and never heard the term made use of before:—sir, it is an unparliamentary word, and you will be laughed at for it;—therefore I desire you will not offer to impose upon me with sic phantoms, but let me know your reason for thus slighting my friends and disobeying my commands.—Sir, give me an immediate and an explicit answer.

Eger. Then, sir, I must frankly tell you, that you work against my nature; you would connect me with men I despise, and press me into measures I abhor; would make me a devoted slave to selfish leaders, who have no friendship but in faction—no merit but in corruption—nor interest in any measure, but their own;—and to such men I cannot submit; for know, sir, that the malignant ferment which the venal ambition of the times provokes in the heads and hearts of other men, I detest.

Sir Per. What are you about, sir? malignant ferment! and venal ambition! Sir, every man should be ambitious to serve his country—and every man should be rewarded for it: and pray, sir, would nai you wish to serve your country? Answer me that.—I say, would nai you wish to serve your country?

Eger. Only shew me how I can serve my country, and my life is hers. Were I qualified to lead her armies, to steer her fleets, and deal her honest vengeance on her insulting foes;—or could my eloquence pull down a state leviathan, mighty by the plunder of his country—black with the treasons of her disgrace, and send his infamy down to a free posterity, as a monumental terror to corrupt ambition, I would be foremost in such service, and act it with the unremitting ardour of a Roman spirit.

Sir Per. Vary weel, sir! vary weel! the fellow is beside himself!

Eger. But to be a common barker at envied power—to beat the drum of faction, and sound the trumpet of insidious patriotism, only to displace a rival,—or to be a servile voter in proud corruption's filthy train,—to market out my voice, my reason, and my trust, to the party-broker, who best can promise, or pay for prostitution; these, sir, are services my nature abhors,—for they are such a malady to every kind of virtue, as must in time destroy the fairest constitution that ever wisdom framed, or virtuous liberty fought for.

Sir Per. Why, are you mad, sir? you have certainly been bit by some mad whig or other: but now, sir, after aw this foul-mouthed frenzy, and patriotic vulgar intemperance, suppose we were to ask you a plain question or twa: Pray, what single instance can you, or any man, give of the political vice or corruption of these days, that has nai been practised in the greatest states, and in the most virtuous times? I challenge you to give me a single instance.

Eger. Your pardon, sir—it is a subject I wish to decline: you know, sir, we never can agree about it.

Sir Per. Sir, I insist upon an answer.

Eger. I beg you will excuse me, sir.

Sir Per. I will not excuse you, sir. I insist.

Eger. Then, sir, in obedience, and with your patience, I will answer your question.

Sir Per. Ay! ay! I will be patient, never fear: come, let us have it, let us have it.

Eger. You shall; and now, sir, let prejudice, the rage of party, and the habitual insolence of successful vice—pause but for one moment,—and let religion, laws, power herself, the policy of a nation's virtue, and Britain's guardian genius, take a short, impartial retrospect but of one transaction, notorious in this land,—then must they behold yeomen, freemen, citizens, artizans, divines, courtiers, patriots, merchants, soldiers, sailors, and the whole plebeian tribe, in septennial procession, urged and seduced by the contending great ones of the land to the altar of perjury,—with the bribe in one hand, and the evangelist in the other,—impiously, and audaciously affront the Majesty of Heaven, by calling him to witness that they have not received, nor ever will receive, reward or consideration for his suffrage.—Is not this a fact, sir? Can it be denied? Can it be believed by those who know not Britain? Or can it be matched in the records of human policy?—Who then, sir, that reflects one moment, as a Briton or a Christian, on this picture, would be conducive to a people's infamy and a nation's ruin?

Sir Per. Sir, I have heard your rhapsody with a great deal of patience! and great astonishment,—and you are certainly beside yourself. What the devil business have you to trouble your head about the sins or the Souls of other men? You should leave these matters till the clergy, wha are paid for looking after them; and let every man gang till the devil his ain way: besides, it is nai decent to find fault with what is winked at by the whole nation—nay, and practised by aw parties.

Eger. That, sir, is the very shame, the ruin I complain of.

Sir Per. Oh! you are vary young, vary young in these matters, but experience will convince you, sir, that every man in public business has twa consciences,—a religious, and a political conscience. Why, you see a merchant now, or a shop-keeper, that kens the science of the world, always looks upon an oath at a custom-house, or behind a counter, only as an oath in business, a thing of course, a mere thing of course, that has nothing to do with religion;—and just so it is at an election:—for instance now—I am a candidate, pray observe, and I gang till a periwig-maker, a hatter, or a hosier, and I give ten, twenty, or thraty guineas for a periwig, a hat, or a pair of hose; and so on, thro' a majority of voters;—vary weel;—what is the consequence? Why, this commercial intercourse, you see, begets a friendship betwixt us, a commercial friendship—and, in a day or twa these men gang and give me their suffrages; weel! what is the inference? Pray, sir, can you, or any lawyer, divine, or casuist, cawl this a bribe? Nai, sir, in fair political reasoning, it is ainly generosity on the one side, and gratitude on the other. So, sir, let me have nai mair of your religious or philosophical refinements, but prepare, attend, and speak till the question, or you are nai son of mine. Sir, I insist upon it.

Enter SAM.

Sam. Sir, my lord says the writings are now ready, and his lordship and the lawyers are waiting for you and Mr. Egerton.

Sir Per. Vary weel: we'll attend his lordship. [*Exit* Sam.] I tell you, Charles, aw this conscientious refinement in politics is downright ignorance, and impracticable romance; and, sir, I desire I may hear no more of it. Come, sir, let us gang down and finish this business.

Eger. [*Stopping Sir* Per. *as he is going off,*] Sir, with your permission, I beg you will first hear a word or two upon this subject.

Sir Per. Weel, sir, what would you say?

Eger. I have often resolved to let you know my aversion to this match.—

Sir Per. How, sir!

Eger. But my respect, and fear of disobliging you, have hitherto kept me silent—

Sir Per. Your aversion! your aversion, sir! how dare you use sic language till me? Your aversion! Look you, sir, I shall cut the matter vary short:—consider, my fortune is nai inheritance; aw mine ain acquisition: I can make ducks and drakes of it; so do not provoke me, but sign the articles directly.

Eger. I beg your pardon, sir, but I must be free on this occasion, and tell you at once, that I can no longer dissemble the honest passion that fills my heart for another woman.

Sir Per. How! another woman! and, you villain, how dare you love another woman without my leave? But what other woman—wha is she? Speak, sir, speak.

Eger. Constantia.

Sir Per. Constantia! oh, you profligate! what! a creature taken in for charity!

Eger. Her poverty is not her crime, sir, but her misfortune: her birth is equal to the noblest; and virtue, tho' covered with a village garb, is virtue still; and of more worth to me than all the splendor of ermined pride or redundant wealth. Therefore, sir—

Sir Per. Haud your jabbering, you villain, haud your jabbering; none of your romance or refinement till me. I have but one question to ask you—but one question—and then I have done with you for ever, for ever; therefore think before you answer:—Will you marry the lady, or will you break my heart?

Eger. Sir, my presence shall not offend you any longer: but when reason and reflection take their turn, I am sure you will not be pleased with yourself for this unpaternal passion. [*Going.*

Sir Per. Tarry, I command you; and, I command you likewise not to stir till you have given me an answer, a definitive answer: Will you marry the lady, or will you not?

Eger. Since you command me, sir, know then, that I can not, will not marry her. [*Exit.*

Sir Per. Oh! the villain has shot me thro' the head! he has cut my vitals! I shall run distracted;—the fellow destroys aw my measures—aw my schemes:—there never was sic a bargain as I have made with this foolish lord,—possession of his whole estate, with three boroughs upon it—six members—Why, what an acquisition! what consequence! what dignity! what weight till the house of

Macsycophant! O! damn the fellow! three boroughs, only for sending down six broomsticks.—O! miserable! miserable! ruined! undone! For these five and twanty years, ever since this fellow came intill the world, have I been secretly preparing him for ministerial dignity,—and with the fellow's eloquence, abilities, popularity, these boroughs, and proper connections, he might certainly, in a little time, have done the deed; and sure never were times so favorable, every thing conspires, for aw the auld political post-horses are broken-winded and foundered, and cannot get on; and as till the rising generation, the vanity of surpassing one another in what they foolishly call taste and elegance, binds them hand and foot in the chains of luxury, which will always set them up till the best bidder; so that if they can but get wherewithal to supply their dissipation, a minister may convert the political morals of aw sic voluptuaries intill a vote that would sell the nation till Prester John, and their boasted liberties till the great Mogul;—and this opportunity I shall lose by my son's marrying a vartuous beggar for love:—O! confound her vartue! it will drive me distracted. [*Exit.*

END OF THE FOURTH ACT.

ACT V. SCENE I.

Enter Sir PERTINAX, *and* BETTY HINT.

Sir Per. Come this way, Betty—come this way:—you are a guid girl, and I will reward you for this discovery.—O the villain! offer her marriage!

Bet. It is true, indeed, sir;—I wou'd not tell your honour a lie for the world: but in troth it lay upon my conscience, and I thought it my duty to tell your worship.

Sir Per. You are right—you are right;—it was your duty to tell me, and I'll reward you for it. But you say Maister Sidney is in love with her too.—Pray how came you by that intelligence?

Bet. O! sir, I know when folks are in love, let them strive to hide it as much as they will.—I know it by Mr. Sidney's eyes, when I see him stealing a sly side-look at her,—by his trembling,—his breathing short,—his sighing when they are reading together. Besides, sir, he has made love-verses upon her in praise of her virtue, and her playing upon the music.—Ay! and I suspect: another thing, sir,—she has a sweetheart, if not a husband, not far from hence.

Sir Per. Wha? Constantia?

Bet. Ay, Constantia, sir.—Lord! I can know the whole affair, sir, only for sending over to Hadley, to farmer Hilford's youngest daughter, Sukey Hilford.

Sir Per. Then send this instant and get me a particular account of it.

Bet. That I will, sir.

Sir Per. In the mean time, keep a strict watch upon Constantia,—and be sure you bring me word of whatever new matter you can pick up about her, my son, or this Hadley husband or sweetheart.

Bet. Never fear, sir. [*Exit*.

Sir Per. This love of Sidney's for Constantia is not unlikely.—There is something promising in it.—Yes! I think it is nai impossible to convert it intill a special and immediate advantage. It is but trying. Wha's there?—If it misses, I am but where I was. [*Enter* Tomlins.] Where is Maister Sidney?

Tom. In the dining room, Sir Pertinax.

Sir Per. Tell him I wou'd speak with him. [*Exit* Tomlins.] 'Tis more than probable.—Spare to speak and spare to speed. Try—try—always try the human heart:—try is as guid a maxim in politics as in war.—Why, suppose this Sidney now shou'd be privy till his friend Charles's love for Constantia.—What then? guid traith, it is natural to think that his ain love will demand the preference,—ay, and obtain it too.—Yes, self—self is an eloquent advocate on these occasions, and seldom loses his cause. I have the general principle of human nature at least to encourage me in the experiment;—for only make it a man's interest to be a rascal, and I think we may safely depend upon his integrity—in serving himself.

Enter SIDNEY.

Sid. Sir Pertinax, your servant.—Mr. Tomlins told me you desired to speak with me.

Sir Per. Yes, I wanted to speak with you upon a vary singular business. Maister Sidney, give me your hand.—Guin it did nai look like flattery, which I detest, I wou'd tell you, Maister Sidney, that you are an honour till your cloth, your country, and till human nature.

Sid. Sir, you are very obliging.

Sir Per. Sit you down, Maister Sidney:—Sit you down here by me. My friend, I am under the greatest obligations till you for the care you have taken of Charles.—The principles—religious, moral, and political— that you have infused intill him, demand the warmest return of gratitude both fra him and fra me.

Sid. Your approbation, sir, next to that of my own conscience, is the best test of my endeavours, and the highest applause they can receive.

Sir Per. Sir, you deserve it,—richly deserve it.—And now, sir, the same care that you have had of Charles,—the same my wife has taken of her favourite Constantia.—And sure, never were accomplishments, knowledge or principles, social and religious, infused intill a better nature.

Sid. In truth, sir, I think so too.

Sir Per. She is besides a gentlewoman, and of as guid a family as any in this county.

Sid. So I understand, sir.

SirPer. Sir, her father had a vast estate; the which he dissipated and melted in feastings, and friendships, and charities, hospitalities, and sic kind of nonsense.—But to the business.—Maister Sidney, I love you,— yes,—I love you,—and I have been looking out and, contriving how to settle you in the world.—Sir, I want to see you comfortably and honourably fixt at the head of a respectable family,—and guin you were mine ain son, a thousand times,—I cou'd nai make a more valuable present till you for that purpose, as a partner for life, than this same Constantia,—with sic a fortune down with her as you yourself shall deem to be competent,—and an assurance of every canonical contingency in my power to confer or promote.

Sid. Sir, your offer is noble and friendly:—but tho' the highest station would derive lustre from Constantia's charms and worth, yet, were she more amiable than love could paint her in the lover's fancy,—and wealthy beyond the thirst of the miser's appetite,—I could not—would not wed her. [*Rises.*

Sir Per. Not wed her! odswunds, man! you surprise me!—Why so?—what hinders?

Sid. I beg you will not ask a reason for my refusal,—but, briefly and finally—it cannot be; nor is it a subject I can longer converse upon.

Sir Per. Weel, weel, weel, sir, I have done,—I have done.—Sit down, man;—sit down again;—sit you down.—I shall mention it no more;—not but I must confess honestly till you, friend Sidney, that the match, had you approved of my proposal, besides profiting you, wou'd have been of singular service till me likewise.—However, you may still serve me as effectually as if you had married her.

Sid. Then, sir, I am sure I will most heartily.

Sir Per. I believe it, friend Sidney,—and I thank you.—I have nai friend to depend upon, but yourself. My heart is almost broke.—I cannot help these tears,—And, to tell you the fact at once—your friend Charles is struck with a most dangerous malady,—a kind of insanity.—You see I cannot help weeping when I think of it;—in short this Constantia, I am afraid, has cast an evil eye upon him.—Do you understand me?

Sid. Not very well, sir.

Sir Per. Why, he is grievously smitten with the love of her;—and, I am afraid, will never be cured without a little of your assistance.

Sid. Of my assistance! pray, sir, in what manner?

Sir Per. In what manner? Lord, Maister Sidney, how can you be so dull? Why, how is any man cured of his love till a wench, but by ganging to bed till her? Now do you understand me?

Sid. Perfectly, sir—perfectly.

Sir Per. Vary weel.—Now then, my very guid friend, guin you wou'd but give him that hint, and take an opportunity to speak a guid word for him till the wench;—and guin you wou'd likewise cast about a little now,—and contrive to bring them together once,—why, in a few days after he wou'd nai care a pinch of snuff for her. [Sidney *starts up.*] What is the matter with you, man?—What the devil gars you start and look so astounded?

Sid. Sir, you amaze me.—In what part of my mind or conduct have you found that baseness, which entitles you to treat me with this indignity?

Sir Per. Indignity! What indignity do you mean, sir? Is asking you to serve a friend with a wench an indignity? Sir, am I not your patron and benefactor? Ha?

Sid. You are, sir, and I feel your bounty at my heart;—but the virtuous gratitude, that sowed the deep sense of it there, does not inform me that, in return, the tutor's sacred function, or the social virtue of the man must be debased into the pupil's pander, or the patron's prostitute.

Sir Per. How! what, sir! do you dispute? Are you nai my dependent? ha? And do you hesitate about an ordinary civility, which is practised every day by men and women of the first fashion? Sir, let me tell you,—however nice you may be, there is nai a client about the court that wou'd nai jump at sic an opportunity to oblige his patron.

Sid. Indeed, sir, I believe the doctrine of pimping for patrons, as well as that of prostituting eloquence and public trust for private lucre, may be learned in your party schools:—for where faction and public venality are taught as measures necessary to good government and general prosperity—there every vice is to be expected.

Sir Per. Oho! oho! vary weel! vary weel! fine slander upon ministers! fine sedition against government! O, ye villain! you—you—you are a black sheep;—and I'll mark you.—I am glad you shew yourself.—Yes, yes,—you have taken off the mask at last;—you have been in my service for many years, and I never knew your principles before.

Sid. Sir, you never affronted them before:—if you had, you should have known them sooner.

Sir Per. It is vary weel.—I have done with you.—Ay, ay; now I can account for my son's conduct—his aversion till courts, till ministers, levees, public business, and his disobedience till my commands.—Ah! you are a Judas—a perfidious fellow;—you have ruined the morals of my son, you villain.—But I have done with you.—However, this I will prophecy at our parting, for your comfort,—that guin you are so very squeamish about bringing a lad and a lass together, or about doing sic an a harmless innocent job for your patron, you will never rise in the church.

Sid. Though my conduct, sir, should not make me rise in her power, I am sure it will in her favour, in the favour of my own conscience too, and in the esteem of all worthy men;—and that, sir, is a power and dignity beyond what patrons, or any minister can bestow. [*Exit.*

Sir Per. What a rigorous, saucy, stiff-necked rascal it is! I see my folly now.—I am undone by mine ain policy.—This Sidney is the last man that shou'd have been about my son:—The fellow, indeed, hath given him principles, that might have done vary weel among the ancient Romans,—but are damn'd unfit for the modern Britons.—Weel, guin I had a thousand sons, I never wou'd suffer one of these English, university-bred fellows to be about a son of mine again;—for they have sic an a pride of literature and character, and sic saucy, English notions of liberty continually fermenting in their thoughts, that a man is never sure of them. Now, if I had had a Frenchman, or a foreigner of any kind, about my son, I cou'd have pressed him at once into my purpose,—or have kicked the rascal out of my house in a twinkling.—But what am I to do?—Zoons! he must nai marry this beggar;—I cannot sit down tamely under that.—Stay,— haud a wee.—By the blood, I have it.—Yes—I have hit upon it.—I'll have the wench smuggled till the highlands of Scotland to-morrow morning.—Yes, yes,—I'll have her smuggled—

Enter BETTY HINT.

Bet. O! sir,—I have got the whole secret out.

Sir Per. About what?

Bet. About Miss Constantia. I have just got all the particulars from farmer Hilford's youngest daughter, Sukey Hilford.

Sir Per. Weel, weel, but what is the story? Quick, quick—what is it?

Bet. Why, sir, it is certain that Mrs. Constantia has a sweetheart—or a husband,—a sort of a gentleman—or a gentleman's gentleman, they don't know which—that lodges at Gaffer Hodges's—and it is whispered all about the village that she is with child by him; for Sukey says she saw them together last night in the dark walk—and Mrs. Constantia was all in tears.

Sir Per. Zoons! I am afraid this is too guid news to be true.

Bet. O! sir, 'tis certainly true, for I myself have observed that she has looked very pale for some time past—and could not eat,—and has qualms every hour of the day.—Yes, yes, sir—depend upon it, she is breeding, as sure as my name is Betty Hint..—Besides, sir, she has just writ a letter to her gallant, and I have sent John Gardener to her, who is to carry it to him to Hadley.—Now, sir, if your worship would seize it— See, see, sir,—here John comes with the letter in his hand.

Sir Per. Step you out, Betty, and leave the fellow till me.

Bet. I will, sir. [*Exit.*

Enter JOHN, *with a Packet and a Letter.*

John. [*Putting the packet into his pocket.*] There—go you into my pocket.—There's nobody in the library, so I'll e'en go thro' the short way.—Let me see, what is the name?—Mel—Meltil—O, no!—Melville, at Gaffer Hodges's.

Sir Per. What letter is that, sir?

John. Letter,sir!

Sir Per. Give it me, sir.

John. An't please you, sir, it is not mine.

Sir Per. Deliver it this instant, sirrah, or I'll break your head.

John. [*Giving the letter.*] There, there your honour.

Sir Per. Begone, rascal.—This, I suppose, will let us intill the whole business.

John. [*Aside..*] You have got the letter, old surly, but the packet is safe in my pocket. I'll go and deliver that, however, for I will be true to poor Mrs. Constantia in spite of you. [*Exit.*

Sir Per. [*Reading the letter.*] Um—um 'and bless my eyes with the sight of you.'—Um—um 'throw myself into your dear arms.' Zoons! 'this letter is invaluable.—-Aha! madam—yes—this will do—this will do, I think.—Let me see, how is it directed—'To Mr. Melville.' Vary weel. [*Enter* Betty.] O! Betty, you are an excellent wench,—this letter is worth a million.

Bet. Is it as I suspected?—to her gallant?

Sir Per. It is—it is.—Bid Constantia pack out of the house this instant—and let them get a chaise ready to carry her wherever she pleases.—But first send my wife and son hither.

Bet. I shall, sir.

Sir Per. Do so—begone. [*Exit* Betty.] Aha! Maister Charles,—I believe I shall cure you of your passion for a beggar now.—I think he cannot be so infatuated as to be a dupe till a strumpet.—Let me see—how am I to act now?—Why, like a true politician, I must pretend most sincerity where I intend most deceit.

Enter EGERTON, *and Lady* MACSYCOPHANT.

Weel, Charles, notwithstanding the misery you have brought upon me,—I have sent for you and your mother in order to convince you both of my affection and my readiness to forgive,—nay, and even to indulge your perverse passion:—for, since I find this Constantia has got hold of your heart, and that your mother and you think that you can never be happy without her, why, I'll nai longer oppose your inclinations.

Eger. Dear sir, you snatch me from sharpest misery;—on my knees let my heart thank you for this goodness.

Lady Mac. Let me express my thanks too,—and my joy;—for had you not consented to his marrying her, we all should have been miserable.

Sir Per. Weel; I am glad I have found a way to please you both at last.—But, my dear Charles, suppose now that this spotless vestal,—this wonder of virtue,—this idol of your heart—shou'd be a concealed wanton after aw,—or shou'd have an engagement of marriage or an intrigue with another man,—and is only making a dupe of you aw this time:—I say, only suppose it, Charles—what wou'd you think of her?

Eger. I should think her the most deceitful, and the most subtle of her sex, and, if possible, would never think of her again.

Sir Per. Will you give me your honour of that?

Eger. Most solemnly, sir.

Sir Per. Enough.—I am satisfied,—You make me young again.—Your prudence has brought tears of joy fra my very vitals.—I was afraid you were fascinated with the charms of a crack.—Do you ken this hand?

Eger. Mighty well, sir.

Sir Per. And you, madam.

Lady Mac. As well as I do my own, sir.—It is Constantia's.

Sir Per. It is so; and a better evidence it is than any that can be given by the human tongue. Here is a warm, rapturous, lascivious letter under the hypocritical syren's ain hand—her ain hand, sir.

Eger. Pray, sir, let us hear it.

Sir Per. Ay, ay;—here—take and read it yourself.—Eloisa never writ a warmer nor a ranker to her Abelard—but judge yourselves.

Eger. [*Reads.*] 'I have only time to tell you, that the family came down sooner than I expected, and that I cannot bless my eyes with the sight of you till the evening.—The notes, and jewels, which the bearer of this will deliver to you, were presented to me, since I saw you, by the son of my benefactor'—

Sir Per. [*Interrupts him by his remarks.*] Now mark.

Eger. [*Reads.*] 'All which I beg you will convert to your immediate use'—

Sir Per. Mark, I say.

Eger. [*Reads.*] 'For my heart has no room for any wish or fortune, but what contributes to your relief and happiness'—

Sir Per. Oh! Charles, Charles, do you see, sir, what a dupe she makes of you? But mark what follows.

Eger. [*Reads.*] 'O! how I long to throw myself into your dear, dear arms; to sooth your fears, your apprehensions, and your sorrows'—

Sir Per. I suppose the spark has heard of your offering to marry her, and is jealous of you.

Eger. Sir, I can only say I am astonished.

Lady Mac. It is incredible.

Sir Per. Stay, stay, read it out—read it out, pray: ah! she is a subtle devil.

Eger. [*Reads.*] 'I have something to tell you of the utmost moment, but will reserve it till we meet this evening in the dark walk'—

Sir Per. In the dark walk—in the dark walk—ah! an evil-eyed curse upon her! yes, yes! she has been often in the dark walk, I believe:—But, read on.

Eger. [*Reads.*] 'In the mean time banish all fears, and hope the best from fortune, and your ever dutiful CONSTANTIA HARRINGTON.'

Sir Per. There—there's a warm epistle for you! in short, the hussy, you must know, is married till the fellow.

Eger. Not unlikely, sir.

Lady Mac. Indeed, by her letter, I believe she is.

Sir Per. Nay, I know she is: but look at the hand—peruse it—convince yourselves.

Eger. Yes, yes, it is her hand; I know it well, sir.

Sir Per. Madam, will you look at it? perhaps it may be forged.

Lady Mac. No, sir, it is no forgery.—Well! after this, I think I shall never trust human nature.

Sir Per. Now, madam, what amends can you make me for countenancing your son's passion for sic a strumpet? And you, sir, what have you to say for your disobedience and your frenzy? O! Charles, Charles—

Eger. Pray, sir, be patient; compose yourself a moment: I will make you any compensation in my power.

Sir Per. Then instantly sign the articles of marriage.

Eger. The lady, sir, has never yet been consulted; and I have some reason to believe that her heart is engaged to another man.

Sir Per. Sir, that is nai business of yours.—I know she will consent and that's aw we are to consider.—O! here comes my lord.

Enter Lord LUMBERCOURT.

Lord Lum. Sir Pertinax, ever thing is ready, and the lawyers wait for us.

Sir Per. We attend your lordship. Where is Lady Rodolpha?

Lord Lum. Giving some female consolation to poor Constantia.—Why, my lady, ha, ha, ha! I hear your vestal has been flirting.

Sir Per. Yes, yes, my lord, she is in vary guid order for any man that wants a wife and an heir till his estate intill the bargain.

Enter SAM.

Sam. Sir, there is a man below that wants to speak to your honour upon particular business.

Sir Per. Sir, I cannot speak till any body now—he must come another time;—hand—stay—what—is he a gentleman?

Sam. He looks something like one, sir—a sort of a gentleman—but he seems to be in a kind of a passion, for when I asked his name, he answered hastily, it is no matter, friend,—go, tell your master there is a gentleman here that *must* speak to him directly.

Sir Per. Must! ha? vary peremptory indeed; pr'ythee, let's see him for curiosity sake. [*Exit* Sam.

Enter Lady RODOLPHA.

Lady Rod. O! my Lady Macsycophant, I am come an humble advocate for a weeping piece of female frailty, wha begs she may be permitted to speak till your ladyship, before you finally reprobate her.

Sir Per. I beg your pardon, Lady Rodolpha, but it must not be: see her she shall not.

Lady Mac. Nay, there can be no harm, my dear, in hearing what she has to say for herself.

Sir Per. I tell you, it shall not be.

Lady Mac. Well, my dear, I have done.

Enter SAM *and* MELVILLE.

Sam. Sir, that is my master.

Sir Per. Weel, sir, what is your urgent business with me?

Mel. To shun disgrace, and punish baseness.

Sir Per. Punish baseness! what does the fellow mean? Wha are you, sir?

Mel. A man, sir—and one, whose fortune once bore as proud a sway as any within this county's limits.

Lord Lum. You seem to be a soldier, sir.

Mel. I was, sir; and have the soldier's certificate to prove my service—rags and scars. In my heart, for ten long years in India's parching clime I bore my country's cause; and in noblest dangers sustained it with my sword: at length ungrateful peace has laid me down where welcome war first took me up,—in poverty, and the dread of cruel creditors.—Paternal affection brought me to my native land, in quest of an only child:—I found her, as I thought, amiable as parental fondness could desire; but lust and foul seduction have snatched her from me, and hither am I come, fraught with a father's anger, and a soldier's honour, to seek the seducer and glut revenge.

Lady Mac. Pray, sir, who is your daughter?

Mel. I blush to own her—but—Constantia.

Eger. Is Constantia your daughter, sir?

Mel. She is; and was the only comfort that nature, fortune, or my own extravagance had left me.

Sir Per. Guid traith, then, I fancy you will find but vary little comfort fra her, for she is nai better than she shou'd be.—She has had nai damage in this mansion. I am told she is with bairn, but you may gang till Hadley, till one farmer Hodges's, and there you may learn the whole story, and wha the father of the bairn is, fra a cheeld they call Melville.

Mel. Melville!

Sir Per. Yes, sir, Melville.

Mel. O! would to heaven she had no crime to answer, but her commerce with Melville.—No, sir, he is not the man; it is your son, your Egerton, that has seduced her; and here, sir, are the evidence of his seduction.

Eger. Of my seduction!

Mel. Of yours, sir, if your name be Egerton.

Eger. I am that man, sir; but pray, what is your evidence?

Mel. These bills, and these gorgeous jewels, not to be had in her menial state, but at the price of chastity.—Not an hour since she sent them— impudently sent them—by a servant of this house—contagious infamy started from their touch.

Eger. Sir, perhaps you may be mistaken concerning the terms on which she received them.—Do you but clear her conduct with Melville, and I will instantly satisfy your fears concerning the jewels and her virtue.

Mel. Sir, you give me new life: you are my better angel. I believe in your words—your looks:—know then, I am that Melville.

Sir Per. How, sir! you that Melville, that was at farmer Hodges's?

Mel. The same, sir: it was he brought my Constantia to my arms; lodged and secreted me—once my lowly tenant—now my only friend. The fear of inexorable creditors made me change my name from Harrington to Melville, till I could see and consult some who once called themselves my friends.

Eger. Sir, suspend your fears and anger but for a few minutes; I will keep my word with you religiously, and bring your Constantia to your arms, as virtuous, and as happy as you could wish her. [*Exit with Lady* Mac.

Sir Per. The clearing up of this wench's virtue is damned unlucky: I am afraid it will ruin aw our affairs again:—However, I have one stroke still in my head that will secure the bargain with my lord, let matters gang as they will. [*Aside.*] But I wonder, Maister Melville, that you did nai pick up some little matter of siller in the Indies; ah! there have been bonny fortunes snapt up there, of late years, by some of the military blades.

Mel. It is very true, sir: but it is an observation among soldiers, that there are some men who never meet with any thing in the service but blows and ill fortune.—I was one of those, even to a proverb.

Sir Per. Ah! 'tis pity, sir, a great pity now, that you did nai get a Mogul, or some sic an animal, intill your clutches. Ah! I should like to have the strangling of a Nabob, the rummaging of his gold dust, his jewel closet, and aw his magazines of bars and ingots. Ha, ha, ha!—guid traith naw, sic an a fellow would be a bonny cheeld to bring till this town, and to exhibit him riding on an elephant: upon honour, a man might raise a poll-tax by him, that would gang near to pay the debts of the nation.

Enter EGERTON, CONSTANTIA, *Lady* MACSYCOPHANT, *and* SIDNEY.

Eger. Sir, I promised to satisfy your fears concerning your daughter's virtue; and my best proof to you, and all the world, that I think her not only the most chaste, but the most deserving of her sex, is, that I have made her the partner of my heart, and the tender guardian of my earthly happiness for life.

Sir Per. How! married!

Eger. I know, sir, at present we shall meet your anger; but time, reflection, and our dutiful conduct, we hope, will reconcile you to our happiness.

Sir Per. Never, never—and could I make you, her, and aw your issue, beggars, I would move hell, heaven, and earth, to do it.

Lord Lum. Why, Sir Pertinax, this is a total revolution, and will entirely ruin my affairs.

Sir Per. My lord, with the consent of your lordship, and Lady Rodolpha, I have an expedient to offer, that will not only punish that rebellious villain, but answer every end that your lordship and the lady proposed by the intended match with him.

Lord Lum. I doubt it much, Sir Pertinax—I doubt it much:—But what is it, sir?—What is your expedient?

Sir Per. My lord, I have another son, and, provided the lady and your lordship have nai objection till him, every article of that rebel's intended marriage shall be amply fulfilled upon Lady Rodolpha's union with my younger son.

Lord Lum. Why that is an expedient indeed, Sir Pertinax.—But what say you, Rodolpha?

Lady Rod. Nay, nay, my lord, as I had nai reason to have the least affection till my cousin Egerton, and as my intended marriage with him was entirely an act of obedience till my grandmother, provided my cousin Sandy will be as agreeable till her ladyship as my cousin Charles here wou'd have been,—I have nai the least objection till the change. Ay, ay! one brother is as guid till Rodolpha as another.

Sir Per. I'll answer, madam, for your grandmother.—Now, my lord, what say you?

Lord Lum. Nay, Sir Pertinax, so the agreement stands, all is right again. Come, child, let us begone.—Ay, ay, so my affairs are made easy, it is equal to me whom she marries.—I say, Sir Pertinax, let them be but easy, and rat me, if I care if she concorporates with the Cham of Tartary. [*Exit.*

Sir Per. As to you, my Lady Macsycophant, I suppose you concluded, before you gave your consent till this match, that there wou'd be an end of aw intercourse betwixt you and me.—Live with your Constantia, madam, your son, and that black sheep there.—Live with them.—You shall have a jointure, but not a bawbee besides, living or dead, shall you, or any of your issue, ever see of mine;—and so, my vengeance light upon you aw together. [*Exit.*

Lady Rod. Weel, cousin Egerton, in spite of the ambitious frenzy of your father, and the thoughtless dissipation of mine, Don Cupid has at last carried his point in favour of his devotees.—But I must now take my leave.—Lady Macsycophant, your most obedient.—Maister Sidney, yours.— Permit me, Constantia, to have the honour of congratulating myself on our alliance.

Con. Madam, I shall ever study to deserve and to return this kindness.

Lady Rod. I am sure you will.—But ah!—I neglect my poor Sandy aw this while! and, guid traith, mine ain heart begins to tell me what his feels, and chides me for tarrying so long.—I will therefore fly till him on the wings of love and guid news;—for I am sure the poor lad is pining with the pip of expectation and anxious jeopardy. And so, guid folks, I will leave you with the fag end of an auld North-Country wish:—'May mutual love and guid humour be the guests of your hearts, the theme of your tongues, and the blithsome subjects of aw your tricksey dreams through the rugged road of this deceitful world; and may our fathers be an example till ourselves to treat our bairns better than they have treated us.' [*Exit.*

Eger. You seem melancholy, sir.

Mel. These precarious turns of fortune, sir, will press upon the heart,—for, notwithstanding my Constantia's happiness, and mine in hers— I own I cannot help feeling some regret, that my misfortunes should be the cause of any disagreement between a father, and the man to whom I am under the most endearing obligations.

Eger. You have no share in his disagreement; for had not you been born, from my father's nature, some other cause of his resentment must have happened.—But for a time at least, sir, and, I hope, for life, affliction and angry vicissitudes have taken their leaves of us all.—If affluence can procure content and ease, they are within our reach.—My fortune is ample, and shall be dedicated to the happiness of this domestic circle.—

My scheme, tho' mock'd by knave, coquet, and fool,
To thinking minds will prove this golden rule;
In all pursuits, but chiefly in a wife,
Not wealth, but morals, make the happy life.

FINIS.